"You've made my life worth living again, Maggie. I'll be forever grateful to you for that." He smiled, and this time it reached all the way to his eyes.

"Grateful?" Maggie stepped back as the smile dropped from her face and apprehension curled in her stomach. "I've just bared my soul to you, and you're *grateful* to me? This is so humiliating."

Jack placed his hands on her shoulders. "I am grateful, Maggie. Because it's made me realise how much I love you and what an idiot I've been in not seeing how much you love me, too."

She looked up at him and met his gaze, seeing the truth in his words. "Would you put another ring on your hand?"

"Only if it's yours," he said, and kissed her.

Molly Evans has worked as a nurse from the age of nineteen. She's worked in small rural hospitals, the Indian Health Service, and large research facilities all over the United States. After spending eight years as a Traveling Nurse, she settled down to write in her favourite place, Albuquerque, New Mexico. Within days she met her husband, and has been there ever since. With twenty-two years of nursing experience, she's got a lot of material to use in her writing. She lives in the high desert, with her family, three chameleons, two dogs and a passion for quilting in whatever spare time she has. Visit Molly at www.mollyevans.com

This is Molly's first book!

THE SURGEON'S MARRIAGE PROPOSAL

BY

MOLLY EVANS

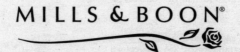

MILLS & BOON

All the characters in this book have no existence outside the imagination
of the author, and have no relation whatsoever to anyone bearing the
same name or names. They are not even distantly inspired by any
individual known or unknown to the author, and all the incidents are
pure invention.

First published in Great Britain 2007
Harlequin Mills & Boon Limited,
Eton House, 18-24 Paradise Road, Richmond, Surrey TW9 1SR

© Molly Evans 2007

ISBN-13: 978 0 263 85253 0

Set in Times Roman 10½ on 12¾ pt
03-0707-46029

Printed and bound in Spain
by Litografia Rosés, S.A., Barcelona

THE SURGEON'S MARRIAGE PROPOSAL

To those who helped me get here:
my family, my friends, the Kick-Ass Sisterhood
critique partners, Gabriella Anderson,
Barbara Simmons and Sheley Wimmer,
the Land of Enchantment Romance Authors,
and my husband, who will always be the hero in my life.

CHAPTER ONE

THE front doors of the Kodiak Island Medical Clinic crashed open and rebounded off the walls. Dr. Jack Montgomery jumped from his chair as an air ambulance crew rushed a patient through. An unfamiliar woman rode the gurney and performed CPR on the fly.

Jack rushed to hold the doors of the trauma room open. "Dammit, Kyle," he barked. "Why didn't you radio? We're not ready for this."

"Couldn't," Kyle said. "Radio's out."

"Ready…to…change," panted the nurse who was performing CPR.

Amos, one of the Alaskan clinic nurses, positioned himself to take over. "Right behind you."

"Ready… Change."

Amos and the air ambulance nurse swapped places without missing a compression.

She jumped down from the gurney, stumbled backward and fell right into Jack. He caught her under the arms and helped her regain her balance, but not before he'd inhaled her fragrance. Musk or sandalwood or something else earthy wafted over him in those few seconds and lingered in his senses.

"What's your name?" he asked as he released her and stepped a pace away.

"Thanks. Just a little wobbly from all the exertion."

"Who are you?" Jack asked again, and looked at the blonde with bright blue eyes and a pink flush to her cheeks.

"Maggie." She sucked in a few deep breaths, recovering from the labor of administering CPR.

"OK, Maggie. What happened to this guy?" Jack asked, starting to examine the man.

"Blunt force trauma to face, chest and abdomen," she said, and pulled her clipboard from beneath the gurney. "A crab pot hit him," she said as a frown of confusion wrinkled her brows.

"He's lucky to still be alive." With his stethoscope, Jack listened to both of the man's lungs. "He's got a pneumo for sure on the left."

"It might be a hemo-pneumothorax with that kind of trauma. He's probably bleeding into the lung, as well as having a collapsed one," Maggie said.

"Probably," Jack acknowledged. "Hold CPR, Amos. Let's check for a rhythm," Jack said.

"V-fib," Maggie said after one look at the monitor. She dashed to the code cart and dragged it to the patient's side.

"Kyle, keep bagging. Amos, resume CPR," Jack instructed. "Maggie, get the defibrillator ready."

"Yes, Doctor." With hands that visibly trembled, she charged the machine. Waiting for it to fully charge took seconds that felt like days, and Maggie's insides tied up in knots.

"Defibrilate, two hundred joules," Jack said.

Maggie tapped a foot as she waited for the beep. "Charged," she said, and pressed the defib paddles to the patient. "Clear!"

Maggie discharged the paddles and the patient spasmed in response.

"Again," Jack said, a muscle twitching in his jaw.

"Charging." Tense seconds passed as the machine recharged and sweat poured down Maggie's back.

First day, first code, first everything. *Welcome to your new job.*

Jack glared at the persistent squiggles on the monitor and started to curse. "Again, dammit," he said, and ran a hand through his hair.

No one breathed as the defibrillator whined. The tension in the air choked Maggie, and she had to draw a deep breath as she hit the button for the third time.

Everyone stared at the monitor. "Asystole," Jack said, his shoulders slumping in defeat as he blew out a long breath. "Damn."

"Give it just a second," Maggie said, and clasped Jack's sleeve, needing a connection to someone, even a stranger, to help get her through this moment. After a few seconds more the monitor blipped and beeped. "Sinus rhythm," she cried, and clapped her hands once. "We did it. Should I start a lidocaine drip?"

"Yes. No. Wait a minute." Jack shook his head and frowned, and had to look away from those blue eyes shining with triumph. He picked up the patient's dog tag. "He's got an allergy to 'caine'-type drugs."

"Bretyllium drip it is," Maggie said, and exchanged the drugs with a happy grin.

"First a bolus, then a drip."

Maggie programmed the IV pump and connected it to the IV site in the patient's arm. "All set, Doctor."

"Jack, please. We're pretty informal around here."

"OK," she said, and dropped her gaze from his, unaccustomed to such familiarity. Maybe it was a sign that things were going to be different for her here.

Jack studied the monitor. "I'm not sure I like his rhythm just yet."

"There's still the collapsed lung," Maggie said, and taped the IV tubes together. "If someone could tell me where the chest tube trays are kept, I'll get one ready," Maggie said.

"Over there." Jack pointed to a supply cabinet and scrubbed at the sink.

"What do you want to use instead of Xylocaine?" Maggie's hands trembled as she searched through the drugs in the code cart. There had to be something else they could use. Did she dare make a suggestion to a doctor who didn't know her or her skills? For a second Maggie bit her lip as she stared at him.

"Something you want to say, Maggie?" Jack asked, and punched his arms into the yellow disposable gown she held out.

"A few milligrams of morphine for pain control and two milligrams of Versed for the sedation and amnesic effects would work."

Jack nodded. "All right. Have you used them before?"

Finally! Something she knew about and could offer without feeling like she was in over her head. "Yes. I'm certified in advanced sedation. Just have to give the Versed slow IV push so the patient doesn't lose his respiratory drive. Same with the morphine."

Jack's glance lingered for a few seconds on her face and a light blush colored it, but she held his gaze.

"That would be bad, wouldn't it?" Jack asked, his eyes crinkling up at the corners.

"Very," Maggie said with a quick smile at his teasing, and then moved to the patient. Maybe this wasn't going to be so bad after all. At least he seemed to have a sense of humor.

"Go ahead, prep him." After giving the sedation Maggie swabbed three quick applications of Betadine solution to the skin. "Ready here," she said, and pulled a blue surgical mask over her face.

"Scalpel."

Maggie slapped a metal scalpel into Jack's palm.

His hand closed around the handle, but he winced behind his protective goggles. "Ouch. Maybe a little lighter next time."

Maggie cringed, a sick feeling twisting tight in her chest. "Sorry. Sorry. God, I'm sorry! First-day jitters."

"It's OK. Just relax. You're doing fine," he said, trying to instill a sense of calmness in her. She was obviously an experienced nurse, but her nerves were overwhelming her.

Maggie took a stack of gauze from her tray and dabbed Jack's forehead before a bead of sweat dripped into his eyes.

"Thanks," he said. "Looks like you've done this before."

"Had a lot of trauma where I came from." When Maggie hooked the collection container to suction, dark red blood drained into it, and a feeling of satisfaction flowed through her. She loved being right, especially when it meant saving a patient.

"Good assessment, Maggie. Clamps and a curved needle, and I'll sew him up."

Jack's simple words of encouragement and approval sent warm heat through her chest as she handed him the instruments. So many times in her last job she'd wished for approval and not gotten it, but here on her first day she'd earned it, mistakes and all. This was going to be a great job.

After Jack had placed a few tight stitches, Maggie stepped closer, her fragrance again washing over him, lingering in his mind and going places he'd thought were locked up tight.

Maggie handed him the appropriate dressing materials in the correct order without him having to say a word. He liked that. Neat, tidy, orderly and mostly calm. Great qualities in a nurse. They would come in handy in this clinic where anything and everything happened twenty-four hours a day. Jack finished applying the tape and patted the dressing. "That ought to do it."

The phone in the room interrupted conversation, and Kyle picked it up. "Plane's here."

After the patient was loaded into the ambulance, Maggie and Jack stood by the clinic doors as it pulled away. He looked down at her until she met his gaze. "You weren't here three weeks ago."

"No. The locum hired me. Today's my first day." She gave a hesitant smile, hoping that he'd approve of the locum's decision. After having come all this way to embark on her first real-life adventure, she'd hate to have to turn around and go back. Then Maggie remembered her resolution. *She'd never go back.*

Jack held out his hand, and she clasped it for a brief moment, but that's all it took for him to feel something tingle in his palm. "I'm Jack Montgomery, the medical director here. Pleased to meet you, Maggie…"

"Wellington."

"Glad to have you on board, Maggie. Welcome to Alaska." He released her hand and opened the door to the clinic, but stopped. "See you later." He turned back into the clinic before he could get lost in those baby blue eyes.

She watched his gait and the rhythm with which he walked and knew instantly that he was a runner.

A sigh of pure female appreciation almost poured from her, but she squelched it. Here and now was not the place or the time to be attracted to anyone, especially the medical director. This was the adventure of a lifetime, and she wasn't going to mess it up.

On her first break in the staff lounge, Maggie reached for the pot of coffee.

"Don't touch that," Jack said from behind her.

Maggie whirled around, her heart fluttering wildly. She placed a hand to her chest with a sigh of relief. "Oh, you startled me."

"Sorry, but I was passing by and wanted to stop you before you poisoned yourself. The coffee is really bad here." Jack entered the small lounge and made it seem smaller.

"Thanks." She returned the Styrofoam cup to the stack.

"I was going to the diner. Care to join me? Coffee's a little better there, but not like in Seattle."

"Caffeine addict?" Maggie asked with a smile, relating to the cravings that hit her every morning.

"Certifiable."

Maggie shoved her hands into her scrub pants pockets as they walked to the ER, hoping that Jack didn't want to take her someplace private to fire her. That would be just her luck, if there'd been a mistake after she'd uprooted her entire life to come here.

At the nurses' station they approached the charge nurse. "Catherine, I'm going to the café, and I'd like to borrow Maggie if you're not too busy here."

"It's pretty slow now, and I'm sure she can use the break, too. I'll page you if anything big comes in."

"So what brings you to Alaska, Maggie?" Jack asked minutes later as they settled into a booth at the café.

"Adventure, I suppose." She smiled up at him, hoping to read something in his face, but his expression remained guarded, watching her as if trying to see inside her brain.

"You're from Boston, right? Aren't there enough adventures in Massachusetts?"

Maggie avoided his glance and fiddled with the handle of her mug. "None that I wanted," she said. "I wanted someplace far from home." Very far.

"You can't get any farther away without leaving the country. What made you leave Boston?"

"I needed a change of pace, change of scenery, change of everything," Maggie said, knowing that was true but leaving out a few details didn't hurt.

"Your résumé said you worked the ER at Massachusetts General Hospital. I'll bet that had plenty of excitement."

"Not the kind I'm looking for," Maggie said, and shook her head, not wanting to think about her time there. "I don't want that any more." She looked up, and her cheeks warmed beneath his probing gaze. Hazel eyes were usually dull, but his were brilliantly colored.

"Where are you staying?"

"There's an inn just down the street, Brownies, that I'm staying in until I can find an apartment or something."

"There are plenty of efficiency apartments around, but they're overpriced during the summer." Jack sipped his coffee but continued to observe her, wondering if she could truly handle it here or if she'd take off when the weather turned cold, like others who had come before her. "Let me ask around and see if there is anyone who might have a place for rent."

"No, you don't have to do that," Maggie asserted. "Really, you shouldn't. I'll find something." She sat up straight and looked at him, concerned he'd go to too much effort on her account and think her nothing but trouble from the start.

"I don't mind," Jack said. He paused and stared into his coffee-cup. "Don't take this the wrong way, but are you planning on staying a while?"

"I don't know. Why?" It would just be her luck if the locum had hired her and Jack didn't approve. "Has there been a mistake in hiring me?" She may as well ask straight out and know right now whether she had a future in Alaska or not.

"No. No mistake. My concern is that I've seen people come to Alaska for a great adventure and leave after a few months. They decide that Alaska is too far, too cold, too something for them, and they return to the lower forty-eight, leaving us with another staffing shortage."

"You're making too many assumptions. I have no intention of leaving," Maggie said, and cocked her jaw to the side, determined to prove him wrong. "I just got here."

"I understand, but as medical director I have to prepare for every outcome, and new staff bolting is one of them," Jack said, his expression grim. "You'll be on probation for sixty days, or until you prove that you can hang in there and aren't going to go back home when things get tough. At the end of your probation we'll re-evaluate."

"I'm not going anywhere, Dr. Montgomery." Maggie leaned back against the red vinyl upholstery of the booth and stared at him.

"Good. But in the meantime we still need to find you some decent housing."

They ordered and ate a simple meal in awkward silence.

"So what about you?" Maggie asked and indicated his left hand. "Wife and kids?"

He looked down and touched his thumb to the simple gold ring he wore. His vows had meant something to him. "No. My wife died before we had children."

"Oh. I'm sorry." Maggie looked away.

Jack stood. He'd heard the words often enough over the years and didn't need to hear them now. "Let's go back to the clinic."

"How long have you been in Alaska?" she asked, hoping she wasn't going to anger him with her questions.

"Six years."

"Did you need to make any adjustments when you came?" She already knew the answer, but had to ask. Something made her curious about Jack, and she wanted to know more.

"Sure, but—"

"So it *is* possible for someone to come from another place to Alaska, and be able to do well here, then?" Maggie slanted a glance at him and waited. She held her breath.

"Yes, of course, you're right—"

"Oh, I love to hear those words. Twice in one day, too." Being right wasn't something that her family credited her with, so she savored the feeling now.

"But, Maggie, I'd planned to come here for years." Jack stopped and stared down at her, his eyes dark and serious.

"How do you know I didn't?" she asked, hoping her pulse would settle down. Confrontations always unnerved her, and she avoided them, but her life depended on this one, and she faced it head-on.

"From what you said, it sounded like an impulse."

"Well, it wasn't. Maybe I didn't plan as long as you did, but this was definitely an intention. I need to be here as much as you do." Probably more, she thought.

"Probation. Sixty days. I'm not changing my mind."

Maggie smiled up at him, and he returned it with obvious reluctance. "OK, but you're going to be eating your words, Jack, and it won't take sixty days."

CHAPTER TWO

JACK left Maggie in the company of Catherine after they returned to the ER. Though it was a small clinic, the flow of patients seemed constant due to the high traffic of village residents, fishermen, and tourists with the occasional fishhook stuck where it wasn't supposed to be.

Two hours later Maggie insisted that Catherine take a break. "Why don't you sit for a while and let me handle the next few who come in?"

"Oh, no, I couldn't," Catherine protested.

Maggie led Catherine to the nurses' station and sat her in a chair. "When are you due?"

"When am I...? How did you know?" Surprise widened Catherine's eyes.

"You've been very discreet, but you've placed your hand over your abdomen several times. Unless you have day-long indigestion, I'd say you're pregnant." Maggie smiled, pleased her observations had been correct and hoping that Catherine wasn't overdoing it.

"You're right. It feels good to tell someone," she whispered.

"No one else knows?" Surprised, Maggie hoped for

an explanation. Having a baby should be something you shouted from the rooftops. Why wasn't Catherine?

"No. I'm only about two months along, and so many things can go wrong in the first trimester." Catherine looked away, but not before Maggie had caught the shine of tears in her eyes.

"Have you had trouble before?" Maggie didn't like to see her new friend suffer, but some women seemed to be plagued with fertility issues. Mother Nature could be a cruel mistress.

Catherine nodded and blew her nose. "Yes. That's why I don't want to say anything. Not until I'm sure this one's a keeper." She patted her abdomen in a protective gesture.

Maggie gave her a quick hug. "I hope so, too. Just take a rest now, will you?"

Catherine dabbed her eyes. "That's what my husband Charlie says, too."

"Well, he's right." Two things Maggie never thought she'd ever have—a husband and a baby—and Catherine had them both. Since her flight to Alaska, her life had already changed for the better. Maybe some day she'd fulfill that dream, too.

"Who's right?" Jack asked as he entered the room, unaware of the intimate conversation between Maggie and Catherine.

Maggie closed her eyes, her heart palpitating in chagrin. How much had he heard? Not much, she hoped. This was Catherine's secret, and Maggie wasn't going to betray it. Her mouth went dry. "Uh, the medical director is always right." She smiled and turned, wide-eyed, to Catherine, hoping she'd go along with it. "Isn't that what you told me?"

"Uh, yeah," Catherine agreed with a choked snort.

He looked back and forth between them, amused doubt shining in his eyes. "I'll believe that when I see it," he said. "Catherine, mind if I borrow Maggie again?"

The women exchanged a glance, and Maggie experienced a measure of relief as the tension in the room evaporated. "Sure, go ahead."

She touched Catherine on the arm, whispering, "I'll be back in a bit. Don't overdo it." Then she turned to Jack. "What are we doing?"

"I know a lady with a room for rent."

"You didn't have to go to the trouble, but I'm grateful."

"I'll take you over and introduce you."

They strolled with silence between them, his loping gait slowed to match hers. Seagulls screeched overhead, looking for any tidbit of food to scavenge, and the breeze whispered softly over her face.

They turned down a narrow street that looked like an oil painting come to life. Every possible color of the rainbow jumped out. Bold reds, the brightest yellows and impossible blues burst from pots and window planters. Even a pair of old boots hanging from a hook boasted an array of playful pansies. "This is lovely," she said, taking in the charm of the street. "It almost doesn't look real."

They walked to a small pink and yellow house at the end of the short row, and Jack knocked on the door. Rubber tires and more old boots had found new life as pansy planters here, too.

"Coming!" The door was yanked open by a gray-haired woman with a pair of striking green eyes. "Hey, there, Doc."

"Ella McGee, meet Maggie Wellington, our newest nurse."

Maggie shook the older woman's hand, smiling into a face filled with the wrinkles of life.

"Nice to meet you," Ella said. "I hear you're looking for a place to stay."

"Yes. Jack said you might have something available." So far so good. Maggie liked the look of the place, warm, inviting, and Ella was friendly enough.

"Come in and have a look," Ella said, and stepped back from the door.

Before Maggie entered the little house, she turned to smile up at Jack. "Thank you. I'm going to like living here." A puzzling warmth flowed through her at Jack's thoughtful gesture. Maybe he didn't think she was going to bolt after all.

Maggie observed Jack during the shift change several hours later. She had been so grateful to him for finding her somewhere to live, and she was certain she had felt something between them as they had walked through the house. But perhaps she was only imagining it. She could only imagine how painful his wife's death must have been. Would he ever consider another relationship? Maggie blew out a sigh and shook her head, trying to clear it. Was his pain any of her concern?

No. She had to prove herself, that's all she had to do, and she had sixty days to do it. Proving herself had been a life-long endeavor, so she was good at it, even when she didn't want to be.

Just then Jack looked up and captured her gaze. Though he was still speaking to a nurse, his piercing gaze remained locked to hers. A vibration charged through her, and her breathing caught as her heart trembled unevenly.

Someone called his name, and his attention turned away from Maggie. The interaction had lasted only seconds, but something intangible and seductive had passed between them. That simple look, that momentary connection, shook her more than she cared to admit. With her head down she took a few deep breaths, clearing her mind and focusing again on the job she had come here to do. Nothing in her plans left room for any sort of liaison, especially with her boss. No lust, no love, no nothing but the job. That was the only thing she could count on.

No, no, no, Maggie. You can't think of that man as anything but your boss.

"Are you OK?"

Maggie turned to face Jack standing beside her, his eyes cool but concerned. The tension that had started to ease rushed back with full force. "I didn't see you come over." Damn. Of all the people in the clinic, it had to be Jack standing there.

"You were hanging on to the desk like there was an earthquake." Jack's sharp gaze moved over her, assessingly.

"An earthquake?" she asked. "Don't tell me I moved to an earthquake zone." Great.

"Out here we're on a fault line bigger than the one in California. Did you feel a tremor just now?"

"I felt something, but I don't know what." Maggie

swallowed and tried to keep her face expressionless. As she stared at him, her mouth went dry.

Jack held her gaze. "Me, too."

Maggie woke in the middle of her first night at Ella's to an emergency call to come in to the clinic. Things that went bump in the night were usually traffic accidents. Bad ones.

Catherine was waiting by the door of the first patient room. "Maggie, go with Jack. I'll take the second patient and get him settled."

Maggie slipped a face shield onto Jack and one on herself. No time for anything else except gloves as the patients came through the doors.

Jack ignored the fluctuation in his heart rate as Maggie's fragrance washed over him, singing through his senses. He was probably just excited about the trauma, that was why his heart beat erratically and why his mouth suddenly went dry.

"Grab a flashlight," he said, and they checked the patient's pupils.

"The left one is sluggish," she said. "Did he hit his head?"

"Yes. I'm worried about a serious brain bleed." Jack looked behind him. "Amos, set up transport to Anchorage."

Sharp footsteps rushed through the ER and arrived at the door of the trauma room. "Where is he? Is he here?" a female voice, bordering on hysteria, cried.

"Oh, dear." Maggie rushed to the doorway to inter- cept the heavily pregnant woman who had just burst in.

Her eyes were wide with shock, and she panted while keeping a hand on her rounded abdomen. "Where is he?" she asked again, and tears flooded her face as she spied a man on a gurney. "That can't be him. Where is he?"

"You're looking for…?"

"Gerald. Gerald Turvick." She sniffed, but the tears still ran.

Maggie curved an arm around the woman's shoulders and took one of her hands. "Are you his wife?"

"Yes," the woman said. "Anita. Now where is he?"

"We're treating Gerald right now. Can you sit outside for just a few minutes while we make him stable?"

"Yes, but where *is* he? I have to know."

The shrill tone of her words scraped Maggie's nerves raw, but she didn't react. The woman was frightened and needed calming comfort right now. "That's him." Maggie gave what she hoped was an encouraging smile, but knew that it couldn't be.

"But look at that man. He can't possibly be my husband."

"Sometimes swelling in the face makes people look different for a while, but it's him." Maggie led Anita to a chair outside the trauma room. "Stay right here for a little while, and I'll come get you as soon as you can see him."

"Was that his wife?" Jack asked when Maggie returned. A muscle in his jaw twitched.

"Yes. You're going to have to talk to her soon. There's no one with her, and she's easily eight months pregnant."

"Great. Just what she needs right now." Jack shook

his head, hating to be the bearer of bad news, but it came with the job. "We'd better talk to her before the transport comes so she can make arrangements. Or something." He felt so helpless when it came to delivering bad news. Every time, he returned emotionally to his wife's illness and the sick feeling in his gut when they had been told the news. The telling never got easier.

They sat beside Anita. "Mrs. Turvick?" Jack asked, and cleared his throat. He reached out for one of her hands. It was ice cold, and he placed his other hand on top of it, hoping to impart a little bit of warmth into her.

"Yes," she whispered as her chin trembled, and her eyes searched Jack's for the truth. "Is he dead?"

"No, but he is seriously injured and is going to need to go to Anchorage for possible brain surgery." It had to be said but, God, he wished there was another way to say it.

"Oh, no," she cried, and covered her face with her hands.

"He's young and physically strong, so those are excellent points in his favor," Jack said, hoping his words would offer her some comfort. But when he'd been told of his wife's illness nothing had helped. Jack's gut twisted into knots as he listened to Anita's sobs. Nothing tortured him more than listening to a woman cry, and as he watched her he froze. Unable to speak, he looked at Maggie.

Sympathy filled her eyes and the sad smile she gave him said she understood his pain.

Something was happening to Jack. She didn't quite know what it was, but there was a plea for help in his eyes. How could she not move to help? That's what she did. She helped people. No matter who they were.

Maggie put an arm around Anita's shoulders and hugged her close.

"That damned man. I told him to sleep more, but when he gets off the boat he wants to sleep in his own bed." She dabbed her eyes. "This was his last trip out before the baby came. Can I see him now?"

Maggie helped Anita to stand and placed a hand on Jack's shoulder. Palpable tension oozed out of him, and he met her gaze. The contact hummed between them as Jack squeezed her hand, then rose. Maybe he needed a friend.

"Dr. Montgomery? Why don't I take Anita in, and you can finish the transport arrangements?" Maggie suggested, then spoke again to Anita. "I'll tell you everything that he's hooked up to so it doesn't frighten you."

"OK, I'm ready," she said, and clutched Maggie's hands as they entered the trauma room, with Jack following behind, feeling useless in the face of the woman's tears and Maggie's obvious control of the situation.

Anita cried softly as Maggie explained everything. As the transport crew arrived Anita leant over his head and kissed his forehead.

Gerald stirred, and his hand moved. Anita grabbed it and held on. "He's squeezing my hand," she cried, and brought his knuckles to her mouth for a kiss.

"He hears you, he really does. He just can't reply with all the tubes in him," Maggie said with tears in her eyes, overjoyed at his response, and she looked at Jack who watched from the doorway. He nodded, his expression grim, and Maggie's heart wrenched. His pain was so overwhelming she could feel it across the room.

"Thank you," Anita said as they left the room. "I

don't know how I'm going to get through this, but if Gerald can be strong, then I can be strong, too."

"Do you have any family or friends who can help you for a while so you're not alone?" Maggie hoped so. Being alone through such a tough time was unthinkable in Anita's condition. If she had no one, Maggie would find a way to help Anita herself.

"Yes, my sister. I don't think I'll be able to go to Anchorage because I'm too close to the due date. I'm sure she'll want to go for me," Anita said, her eyes bright with new hope.

"Why don't you go home now?" Maggie suggested.

"I will and thank you again." Anita hugged Maggie to her.

Maggie watched as Anita left and sensed Jack beside her. "I hope he makes it," she said, and heaved a sigh as they re-entered the clinic after the patient had been transported.

"Think you're up to a lifetime of this?" Jack asked as they entered the staff lounge.

Maggie let out a quick laugh, letting the tension of the last few hours drop away from her. "A lifetime? Let me get through the first week, OK?"

"Fair enough." Jack's lips made an effort to smile, but the gesture didn't reach his eyes.

He dropped into the couch with a sigh and rubbed his face in his hands.

Maggie watched him a few moments. She wanted to go to him, offer him a shoulder in friendship, but was that overstepping the boundaries between boss and employee? She offered comfort all the time to strangers. What was stopping her from reaching out to Jack?

Maggie sat down and blew out a long breath. "That was tough, wasn't it?" she asked, and hoped that he'd respond, not shut her out.

"I think he's going to make it."

"I meant telling the wife about her husband." As soon as she'd said it, Maggie bit her lip, hoping Jack didn't take her head off for probing into his pain.

Jack sat up. After a moment he spoke. "Yes." He turned and looked at her. "Yes, it was hard."

"Want to talk about it?" Maggie cringed a little, waiting for Jack to respond.

"No." He shook his head and looked away. "Thank you," he added in a hoarse whisper.

Maggie's heart was breaking for Jack and the pain he'd suffered, still suffered, and couldn't seem to share. "Well, if you ever need to talk, I'm here, Jack." At least she had offered and now it was up to him whether he'd reach out or not.

Jack nodded, patted Maggie once on the knee and left the lounge.

The day passed with unusual slowness compared to the busy pre-dawn. By noon Maggie was yawning at the triage desk when Jack approached. "I've asked another nurse to come in for a few hours so you can go home."

"Did I do something wrong?" Panicked, she jumped up from behind the desk, not wanting to disappoint him. So many times she'd been a disappointment to her family—she didn't want to be one here, not when probation loomed over her head and the potential loss of her job. "Whatever I did, I'm sorry," Maggie panted as she stared at Jack.

"Whoa, Maggie, slow down. You haven't done

anything wrong." He moved toward her and placed his hands on her shoulders.

"Don't treat me differently because I'm on probation."

"I'm not. Calm down. I'd do this for any of the staff. Catherine's gone home, why shouldn't you?"

Maggie stared at Jack as her heart palpitated in her chest. Slowly she unclenched her hands, which she hadn't realized were knotted in front of her. After a deep sigh the sweat trickling down her back stopped. The fist in her gut evaporated, too. Why had she reacted so strongly? Old fears haunted her and surfaced when she wasn't holding them back. "God, Jack. I'm sorry." She sent an apologetic glance his way and was relieved to see a calm expression on his face.

Jack smiled lopsidedly. "You're just tired. Why don't you go home and get some sleep? It's been a rough shift."

"I'm OK. A few more cups of coffee and I'll be good for the rest of the shift." Another yawn caught her off guard, and she clamped a hand over her mouth.

"You know, if you suppress a yawn it leaks out your ears," Jack said, not taking his eyes off of her.

Maggie snorted a laugh and dropped her hand. "It does not." She thought a second and then narrowed her eyes at Jack. "Does it?"

Jack gave a quick laugh. "If you're even considering it, you're too tired. Go home, have a nap. If you're up for it later, I'll give you a tour of the island." Keeping his eyes on the chart, he didn't look up as he made the offer.

"I'd like that."

Jack sensed the pleasure in her voice and watched her leave. Why had he made such an offer? But how could he retract it now without feeling like an idiot? He sighed and headed to his office, irritated with his impulsive gesture. Rubbing a hand over his face, he groaned. After locking the door to his office, Jack went home, too.

That evening, while the sun still blazed high overhead, looking much like a pleasant afternoon, Maggie explored the village of Kodiak. After meandering down a side street crowded with quaint gift shops carrying Alaskan-made foods and gifts, she started back toward Ella's. Maggie didn't consider it her home yet, because it wasn't.

That was another thing she'd need to think about—calling someplace home, putting down roots and establishing herself in a community. She'd volunteered at several charities in Boston. Maybe she could find some place in Kodiak to volunteer, too.

As she wandered in and out of stores, Maggie made several purchases and tucked the bags under her arm. Kodiak was a lovely village, and she was happy she'd come here. Perhaps one day she'd call this place home.

When she got back to the cottage, after putting her purchases away, she looked at the answering-machine and stifled a blip of disappointment that Jack hadn't called. Then the phone rang and her heart pulsed with anticipation as she picked it up.

"Hello? McGee residence."

"Hi, Maggie. It's Jack."

When he spoke her name, she paused. The quiet of

the line and the empty house lent an unexpected intimacy. She shivered. *Focus, Maggie. Focus.*

"Hello, Jack. H-how are you?"

"I slept for a few hours, so I'm ready for another round. You?"

"Oh." Disappointment chased away the initial excitement his call had inspired. "Is there another emergency I need to come in for?"

"No, everything's quiet at the clinic. I meant the island tour. You still interested?"

Pleasure pulsed in a throbbing wave. *So much for focus.* She switched the phone from one ear to the other, but her suddenly moist hand slipped on the receiver. It bounced off the counter and clattered to the floor. Horrified, she scooped up the phone and clutched it to her ear. "I'm so sorry, Jack! I dropped the phone." She cringed, even though he couldn't see her. Chalk up another mistake to her growing list of them.

"If you didn't want to go, all you had to do was say no," Jack said. "You didn't have to deafen me in the process."

Maggie heard the smile in his voice, and gave a relieved laugh. "I'd love to go."

"See you in ten, then."

After a quick change into a fresh shirt, she grabbed a light jacket and waited on the porch for Jack. In minutes the squeak of brakes alerted her to his arrival. Maggie stuffed her jacket in the back seat and reached to buckle her seat belt, but it resisted the efforts of her suddenly trembling fingers.

"It sticks sometimes," Jack said, and placed his hand over hers.

Startled, Maggie looked up as he leaned toward her. His mouth neared hers. Anticipation flooded her as her lips parted. Then Jack pulled back with a can of oil in one hand, which he had grabbed from under the seat.

"Just needs a little coaxing," he said.

The quick spurt of pressurized oil made Maggie jump and the belt snapped into place. "Oh," she said, trying to forget the way she had just thought about kissing Jack. "It scared me."

He gave a wicked grin. "Wait till you see me drive."

CHAPTER THREE

"SO, WHERE are we going?" Maggie asked, eager to see more of the island and have the wind blow away any intimate thoughts of Jack. Getting cozy with the boss wasn't in her plans. Not now, not ever, despite the budding attraction she had for him. He wasn't available. She couldn't believe that he was still emotionally attached to his deceased wife. How did a woman compete with that anyway?

"There's a lot to see. Want to just drive around for a while?"

"Sure."

Jack drove out of town where the road paralleled the inlet. Maggie watched as a pod of killer whales made their way through the water. "Oh, how magnificent!" Maggie cried. "I've never seen a group of whales like that. Can we stop?" Without thinking, she clutched Jack's sleeve.

"We can stop at the viewing station up ahead." Maggie's excitement blossomed in her cheeks and left a sparkle in her eyes. Jack was captured by the spell, powerless to resist her charm.

"Thank you, Jack," she said. "I've only seen them in captivity, never like this."

Before Jack had pulled off to the side of the road Maggie had unbuckled her seat belt and almost dove from the Jeep. A large orca breeched, shooting out of the water and landing on its back, splashing water higher than any building on the island.

She stood breathless, awed by the power of the whale and the roar of the splash. Tears came to her eyes at the overwhelming sight. Never in her life had she seen such a beautiful thing. Never had she been allowed the freedom to explore. As she stood beside Jack and watched the group of killer whales feed just yards from shore, she realized her past was behind her—she just had to keep it that way. Breathless, she turned to Jack. "This is just remarkable. Do you see this every day?" she asked, emotion choking her voice.

"No, not every day, but frequently. They summer here." Jack watched her. The excitement in her eyes pleased him, as if he had brought her there for just this moment, as if knowing the whale was going to perform just for her. He'd almost forgotten how powerful the animals were, but now, watching them through Maggie's eyes, the wonder was almost new again.

The breeze pulled a lock of hair from her ponytail and teased her cheek with it. Just as Jack reached out to tuck the lock away, Maggie's hand moved to do the same. Their hands collided, and Jack pulled back as if stung.

"I'm sorry. I shouldn't have…" Jack's voice trailed off. What was the matter with him?

"Shouldn't have what?" she asked.

"Tried to, um…push your hair back. I used to do that… I didn't…" He felt like a schoolboy with the embarrassment of first attraction. Was that what this was? Attraction? Wanting to touch Maggie? "It was inappropriate of me. I'm sorry." Jack shoved his hands into his pockets and faced the water. It was safer than facing Maggie.

"It's OK, Jack. I understand. Old habits." She turned back to watch the whales, seemingly undisturbed by it.

Jack nodded and cleared his throat. "Let's get going," he said.

"Can I ask you a personal question?" Maggie asked as they drove along.

"Do we know each other well enough for personal questions?" Jack asked, a frown darkening his expression.

"We're going to." She really wanted to know. This wasn't just polite conversation. Jack interested her, despite her efforts not to be attracted to him.

"OK, what do you want to know?"

"What happened to your wife?" The question was seemingly rude, but there was no simple way to ask, and she hoped she didn't alienate their developing friendship by being too personal too quickly.

"She had ovarian cancer. She was twenty-eight."

Maggie gasped and in an instant wished she hadn't asked the question. "She was so young. I'm sorry."

"Yes, she was."

Maggie clenched her hands in her lap, unsure of what to do with them. She wanted to reach out to him, but she didn't. A muscle twitched in Jack's jaw, and he stared ahead at the road, his expression closed off, and Maggie sighed. To try to console him, even with a light squeeze on his shoulder, was too personal, so she opted for a lighter mood and a different subject. "OK, tour guide, give me some history on this tour, will ya?"

Jack slid her a sideways smile, and she knew she had pleased him with the change of topic. As he talked, his shoulders relaxed, and he rested his wrist casually over the steering-wheel.

"There's a great little dive that I'd like to take you to, if you don't mind." He looked at her and his eyes were calm, the turmoil of emotions now gone.

Maggie gave a quick laugh, relieving any lingering tension between them. "In my experience, *great* and *dive* aren't usually used in the same sentence. I take it you've eaten here before and survived."

Jack grinned. "Many times."

After they were seated, Maggie looked at the menu and they shared drinks. "I'm not sure what to have. It all sounds good."

"This is your first trip to Alaska. You've got to have salmon." After the waiter had taken their order Jack spoke. "So, Maggie, tell me your story."

Maggie looked into his eyes, but didn't suffer any anguish at what could have been an uncomfortable question. Gone was the interrogation of the medical director. This was something different. Reading people's eyes came as second nature to her, both in her job and in her family. Something deeper motivated Jack, and he was really interested in the answer.

"My story?" Before answering, she looked away from the intensity of his gaze and ran one finger around the rim of the glass.

"Yeah. Everyone's got a story," he said, and sipped his wine.

He'd offered her a gesture of friendship, and she took it. She had to trust sometime. "If I had stayed where I was, I would have died."

"Were you sick?"

"Yes. Sick of the life I was living, having my life micromanaged by my father. I had been searching the journals and online ads for jobs, but nothing sounded right until I found this job. I handed in my notice, hopped a plane, and here I am."

"Just like that?"

"Just like that." Maggie saluted him with her wineglass and took a long drink. "When something is right, you know it. And when it's wrong, you know that, too."

"How so?" Jack focused his entire attention on her.

Maggie trembled a little under the intensity of his gaze, but went on. "Because my entire life has been dictated by my father. I've always been a project to him, never a person who might have needs or wants of her own. And I did." She shook her head, correcting herself. "I do. The time had come for me to make a break from a life that was killing me. Simple as that." She huffed out a quick breath and took a gulp of her drink as fiery heat overtook her cheeks. She hated it when it her emotions betrayed her.

"I'm sorry if I made you uncomfortable. That wasn't my intention."

"Well, now you know the deep dark truth about Maggie Wellington," she said, and looked away.

"Maggie?"

"Yes?" Here it came. The let-down. Hating to do it,

she looked up anyway, and met Jack's gaze. There was nothing but a friendly light shining in it.

"It's not that deep or dark."

"I won't disappoint you, Jack. I promise."

Her face brightened, and Jack was glad to see it. He knew she had worried about his expectations, but trying to put her at ease had only seemed to make her anxiety worse.

"There are many things I don't know about frontier medicine, but every day I'm learning more, and I won't let you down." Eagerness tore through her. "Why don't you tell me about some of the unusual cases that come in? I'd love to hear about them," she said, as the waiter arrived with their meal of blackened salmon on a bed of angel-hair pasta for both of them.

"If you don't mind while we eat." Jack hesitated.

She waved away his concern. "Please. I'm a nurse. We talk about bowel surgery while eating sausage."

Jack described some of the cases that had come through the clinic doors. Things Maggie never would have experienced anywhere else.

"And then a native family came in with a massive case of food poisoning from eating fermented beaver tail," Jack said, and speared a chunk of salmon.

Maggie quit eating and placed a hand to her throat. "OK, stop. Now you're going to make me sick," she said, and sipped her wine.

"Sorry." He laughed. "But I warned you."

"I know. Try another story that's less descriptive, will you?" She shivered as Jack moved on to another, less nauseating story.

Sated, they returned to Kodiak in a companionable

silence. As they drove along, Maggie watched for more whales, hoping to see more of those wondrous creatures. A strange movement at the edge of the receding water caught her eye. "What's that? Another group of whales?" She pointed to the area past the viewing point they had stopped at earlier.

"The tide's gone out," Jack said, and swung the vehicle into the parking area, his curiosity also aroused. "Let's take a closer look."

They hurried to the viewing platform and hung over the side, trying to get a better look. "It's a whale in the mud!"

"Sometimes they beach themselves when they lose direction or follow a school of fish in too far." Jack didn't want to think how Maggie would react to this after seeing them in the wild for the first time.

"That's terrible. Can we help it?" The danger the whale was in overwhelmed the wonder of the previous sighting.

Jack led her to a gate, the concern in her voice urging him on. "I think we can get through over here. I'll help you over the rocks." Maggie followed, clutching his arm. "Don't go too far in. People digging for clams or walking out on the tide flats have gotten stuck."

"Really?" Maggie backed away from the mud, her eyes wide.

"Yes, and when the tide came back in again, they drowned."

The magic in Maggie's eyes was fading quickly to horror. "You're serious?"

"Very. That's why it's good to explore with someone who knows the area."

"What can we do to help the whale? I don't want to just stand here and watch it die."

Maggie's gaze bored into his, and he was helpless against the plea. Jack looked at the huge animal as it thrashed, trying to right itself. It was still half-covered by water, but it would be completely exposed when the tide receded.

"I don't know anyone at Fish and Game, but Ella will." Jack pulled out his cell phone. Not only was it important that they get help for the beached whale, but also for some reason he wanted to help the animal for Maggie. She was the first woman he'd been attracted to since his wife's death. That meant something, didn't it? She cared about people and animals, that was obvious. Though he couldn't physically or emotionally reach out to her, he could do this. That was the most he could give her.

Dialing the number Ella gave him, Jack clenched his jaw, irritated that his thoughts had strayed to any sort of romantic liaison with Maggie. He took a few steps away from her, needing a little space to clear his head. Aside from his commitment to his vows, he was Maggie's boss. How irresponsible could he be, allowing himself to be attracted to her?

"Thanks," Jack said, and ended the call. "Fish and Game will be here soon. They'll know what to do."

Maggie clutched Jack's arm briefly then released it. The whale no longer thrashed about but lay still in the water, having exhausted its energy. Maggie pointed to a place farther out in the inlet where spouts of water flew high in the air. "Look. More whales."

"They're probably family to this one. From what I

know about orcas, they travel in family pods. This could be a young whale that got separated from his family, and they're out there, waiting for him to come back."

Jack went to fetch a bucket from the Jeep and returned to Maggie. "Don't get near its head. It may try to bite you out of fear, and those teeth could take off your leg."

"OK." She stepped back. "Look at the tide. I can't believe how fast it moves."

Jack could hear the fear in her voice, and he cringed inwardly. "Don't worry. F and G will be here soon. But, Maggie," he warned her, hating to dampen that beautiful light in her eyes but unable to lie about the risks, "sometimes Mother Nature can be harsh. The whale may not live, not even with all the help we can give it."

Solemnly she nodded, her mouth turned down. "I know, but we have to try, don't we?"

There was no doubt in Maggie, and her courage urged him on. "We do."

Together they approached the orca, now almost completely exposed by the receding tide. Maggie stroked its dorsal fin, affection and concern for the animal obvious. "You're going to be OK, baby," Maggie said, and stroked it once more. They filled the container with seawater and poured it over the whale, bathing the animal's skin. Though late in the evening, the sun was still high in the sky, and the whale would dry out quickly.

Three hours later, exhaustion overcame Maggie. F and G officials finally arrived, but they couldn't do anything more than what Jack and Maggie had done. Mother Nature would take its course.

"This is so frustrating," Maggie said, her hands clenched into fists at her side. "We should be doing more. Isn't there something else we can do?"

Jack looked across the whale at her. Tears filled her luminescent blue eyes, and he wanted to go to her, offer her comfort, but he couldn't. Could he? What stopped him? The ring of gold burning on his left hand?

Maggie turned away and wiped her eyes. Without thinking, he walked around the whale and pulled her into his arms. "It'll be OK, Maggie," Jack whispered. "It's OK." Too many emotions churned inside him to be held back. Jack had been dead inside for a long time. But now, standing in the mud, holding Maggie as the glorious midnight sun set, he was coming alive.

For a minute or two she clung to him, then she pushed back. "I'm sorry. I must really be tired." Maggie wiped her face on her sleeve. She had to be strong in front of Jack, show him she could take it here, not fall to pieces in an emergency, even if it was an animal emergency.

"You're not blubbering, and I'm not sorry. Not sorry at all," Jack said. He wanted to keep her in his arms, but he let her move away. It was safer that way.

"I guess we'd better get back to town, but I hate to leave in the middle of this," Maggie said. She dropped her hands to her sides and lowered her gaze to her boots.

Jack ran his hand down the tangle of her hair blown wild by the wind. He squeezed both of her arms and then tipped her face up. He gave her a gentle smile and was rewarded with a curve of her lips, but sadness still swirled in her eyes.

Looking at her, something shifted inside him. For a

second he pondered his wedding band, then his gaze returned to her.

She didn't even know yet how long she'd be staying in Kodiak. How could he be starting to have feelings for her? He'd only known Maggie Wellington a few days and certainly not well enough to embrace her or imagine kissing her. She came from money and was used to grander surroundings than a small village like Kodiak. When the novelty of living here wore off, she'd move on to bigger and better things than this island and he could offer. A man without emotion was nothing inside. And that's all he was.

Maybe that was just an excuse on his part. Shoving his clenched fists into his pockets, he walked out onto the mud flat and stared at the sea. After Arlene had died he'd thought about walking onto the flats and letting the tide take him. But something, some sense of responsibility to his community and his profession, had held him back.

The whale exhaled and redirected Jack's attention from his maudlin thoughts. He strangled his emotions, pushing them back where they belonged.

"Is there anything else we can do?" he asked one of the rescuers.

"No, but thanks for the help. We'll be at this until the morning tide turns," he said.

Jack looked at Maggie in her muddy and bedraggled state. "What do you think? Is this enough adventure for one day?" Jack asked.

Maggie gave a tired nod. "What a night," she said as they returned to the parking lot.

"This wasn't quite the drive around the island I

expected." Jack smiled at her, liking the look of her sleepy face. She would look like that after spending a passionate night in her lover's arms. Jack clenched his jaw and wished he could squash his thoughts as easily.

"I guess we'd better get back," Maggie said, and covered a yawn with the back of her hand. "I'm beat."

The silent drive lulled Maggie nearly to sleep. At four a.m., Jack pulled up at Ella's door with a squeak of brakes and made a mental note to get them checked.

Maggie faced Jack, her eyes barely open. "Thanks for the tour."

"You're welcome. Next time maybe it won't be quite such an adventure."

"I'm glad we helped the whale, though." She moved to an upright position and kept her gaze locked with his. "I hope it lives."

Without understanding why, Jack took her hand. A scar on the middle finger could have marred the perfect skin, but most people wouldn't have noticed it. Jack's thumb traced the tiny raised line. "What happened here?"

Maggie looked at the spot. "Oh, I got carried away with a large vegetable knife, trying to chop like the chefs on television. Cut it to the bone." She smirked at her own stupidity. "Hurt like the blue blazes, too."

Jack raised her hand and kissed the scar then, without thinking, pulled her close and kissed her lips. Exploring their dewy softness pulled a thread of desire taut in his belly, and almost unraveled the control he kept wound tight. As she opened her soft mouth beneath his, his tongue tasted the lingering freshness of the sea, and Jack savored the feel of her against him. Lord help him, but he wanted her. He really wanted to take her home and make love to her, but it would be a dreadful mistake. Until Maggie showed up, he'd almost forgotten what desire felt like. Emotions and physical needs only complicated life, and Maggie unleashed both of those in him. He pulled back with an apology.

"I'm sorry." Jack placed one small kiss on her forehead as he breathed in her fragrance and tried to still the beating of his heart, desire still pumping through his veins.

"Don't worry. We're both tired." Maggie's arms held on to him, and her breathing was as uneven as his.

"But I shouldn't have…"

"It was a kiss, Jack. That's all." She touched his cheek with her palm.

"OK. See you tomorrow." Jack nodded and released her.

Maggie slid from the seat and entered the house.

He was unable to offer Maggie a relationship. So why bother to think about having one with the most interesting woman to wander into his life in a long time? They could have an affair, a lovely, passionate, glorious affair, but in the end they'd both get hurt. That pain could be avoided simply by not becoming involved in the first place and keeping his emotional distance.

After the short drive home, Jack entered his quiet house. After being with Maggie, his home suddenly looked drab and pale. Too tired to think, he stripped and fell onto the bed. Dreams came in swirling mists that clouded his mind, leaving behind the memory of soft curves and passionate kisses.

CHAPTER FOUR

MAGGIE struggled into a light jacket and bolted from the house with a bagel clamped in her mouth. Coffee would just have to wait until she got to the clinic.

The clock showed one minute before seven a.m. as she signed in for her shift. Angry voices from one of the patient rooms forced Maggie to abandon her breakfast on the desk, and she hurried to investigate the disturbance.

Jack stood beside a gurney with an angry fisherman on it who struggled to get up, flailing his legs and arms in all directions. The fisherman looked like a plaid turtle that had landed on his back. "I don't need no goddamn stitches," he yelled. He took a swipe at Jack, but the man was too drunk to aim well, and Jack moved too quickly.

"Hey, sailor, what's going on?" Maggie asked the patient. She strolled into the exam room, ignoring Jack for the moment.

"He's poking needles in my face," the man cried to Maggie. "Help me. I don't like needles," he said, sounding like a youngster who had just been told to eat his broccoli.

"Well, why don't you look at me instead of at that nasty needle? Don't worry, the doctor is a real expert stitcher." Maggie sat on the edge of the gurney and took the man's hand in hers.

"Lookin' at you's a whole lot better than looking at him," he said, darting a quick glare in Jack's direction.

"Concentrate on my eyes and listen to the sound of my voice, and everything will be fine," she said in a soothing tone. She continued in a soft monotone, reciting a silly rhyme she'd learned as a girl.

Jack flashed a grin at her and went to work, stitching the gaping laceration over the man's left eye. The man never moved, except to allow his eyes to drift downward, and his breathing eased into snoring grunts. Just as Jack finished and snipped the thread, the man's hand went limp in Maggie's.

"Nice work," Jack said, his brows raised in amazement. "You hypnotized him."

Maggie stood and adjusted a sheet over the slumbering drunk. "Me and Jack Daniels." Maggie sighed in relief. "Relaxation techniques can work wonders."

"I see they do. Your approach was great. I was halfway to calling for some muscle to hold him down, and you did the job in ten seconds with no effort at all." Jack slapped a hand on the desk, enormously pleased with the outcome of the situation.

"I disagree. It was an effort," Maggie said.

"How? It didn't look like it."

Maggie enjoyed putting the confusion in Jack's eyes. "I had to say something nice about you. You don't know how hard that was." Maggie grinned and jumped back as Jack tossed a wadded-up towel at her.

"Smart ass," he said and chuckled. "We'll let him sleep some of this off."

"OK. I'll get report from the other shift and see you later." But she cast a glance over her shoulder and hesitated. Her gaze met his and held for a long moment. Another nurse called to Maggie, and she hurried to the report room. "Coming!"

Jack watched as she left the treatment room. She had really amazed him with that trick. Holding down a drunk was no easy task, but Maggie had accomplished it with the touch of her finger. He wondered how many other men she had wrapped around those fingers. The dull blast of water into the metal sink sounded hollow and jolted him from his mental musings. *What an idiot I am to think of Maggie in that way.* He saw the silent questions in her eyes before she left the room. Even though she had said the kiss was nothing, she wanted to know what was between them. He wondered himself. He'd spent half of the previous day berating himself for giving in to his attraction to her. And he'd spent the other half thinking about how good she'd felt in his arms. If he closed his eyes and thought about it, he could almost taste her lips again, smell the sea in her hair and feel the future in her arms.

The squawk of the radio drowned out his daydream, and he sighed, picked up the microphone and spoke to the air ambulance.

"Kodiak base. November romeo eight zero eight zero. Go ahead."

"Jack? This is Kyle. We've got a bad one coming in."

"What is it?"

"Bear mauling," Kyle said.

Jack blew out a breath. "What's your ETA?"

"Thirty minutes."

"We'll be ready." Jack signed off.

He gathered the staff to prepare them for the case coming in, but Maggie wasn't there. Irritation made a tight knot in his jaw. This had better not be the time she went AWOL on him. He dismissed the staff and entered the clinic's waiting area. "Excuse me, everyone," he called, and all of the patients looked at Jack. "We're really in for a bad case that's going to require all of our attention for a while. If any of you can wait for a few hours, please, go home and come back after lunch. I apologize for the inconvenience." There were a few stifled coughs and covered sneezes, but no one complained. They all knew that in a small community such things happened. Everyone rose to leave. "Thanks. We'll get to you as soon as we can," he said, and turned to go.

"What you got coming?" one crusty old salt asked. He rose on bowed legs that didn't look as if they would hold his weight and held on to the chair with gnarled hands, disfigured by rheumatoid arthritis.

"Bear mauling," Jack answered and took the man's arm to assist him to the door. "Tom, are you having trouble that can't wait?" Jack asked as he noticed Tom's unusually slow gait.

"No." He pulled a zipper bag filled with prescription bottles and shook it once. "Just need to get me some refills."

"Do you want to leave the bag? I can have one of the nurses call in the refills."

"No. I'll just head to the diner for a bit and come back later. You don't need a crippled old man distracting you right now." Tom patted Jack on the sleeve and shuffled his way out of the clinic. Reaching down to grasp the handle of a beaten old red wagon filled with discarded cans and bottles Tom had collected along the way, he made his way across the street to the diner.

Jack's attention returned to the situation at hand. *Where the hell was Maggie?* Jack returned to the trauma room and jerked back the curtain to find Maggie, dressed in protective gear. A face shield lay on the counter, and the entire room was set up for a critical trauma.

"What's going on, Maggie? Who did all this?" Stupefied, he entered the room.

"I did." She slid an intubation tray onto the counter.

"You weren't there when I made the announcement to the staff."

"I heard your conversation on the radio. I didn't realize you were having a press conference about it," she said, and held out a gown for him to put on. Jack placed his arms in the sleeves, and Maggie tied the gown at the back.

"But...how...?"

"As soon as you signed off the radio I came in here to get the room ready. At least as ready as I could. If there's something I haven't thought of, tell me, and I'll get it ready." After ripping open the sterile gloves, she held each one out for him to shove his hands into. "Hell, Jack. Did you think I'd run away or something?" she asked.

The flush creeping up Jack's neck answered for him. With her lips pressed tightly together, she placed the face shield over his ears. Unable to avoid his gaze, she looked at him and could see the apology in his eyes, but it wasn't enough to soothe the hurt. As he opened his mouth to speak, the patient and flight crew burst through the doors.

"He's not looking good, Jack." Kyle, one of the flight crew, reported. "I've got him as high as I can go on oxygen. You're going to have to intubate him so we can control his airway better."

Jack listened to the man's lungs. "He's really tight." He turned to Maggie. She was already opening the intubation tray. She just knew, seemed to read his thoughts as she sprang into action, anticipating his every need.

Maggie held up a syringe. "Ready with succsinyl-choline when you are," she said.

"Dammit, Maggie. You're such a good nurse you're taking all the fun out of having to tell you what to do next," Jack said. "Go ahead."

Maggie injected the medicine that would temporarily paralyze the patient's vocal cords into the IV line, making the procedure easier. "If you have any trouble, I'm pretty good at intubation," she offered.

"I hope we won't need it, but thanks. Glad to know it."

"Ready with ten milligrams of Valium as well," Maggie said.

"Valium, OK," Jack said as he inserted the tube through the now paralyzed vocal cords and into the patient's lung. "Respiratory, bag him."

"I'm on it," the respiratory therapist said. "There's a ventilator set up and waiting."

"Good," Jack said. "Maggie, assess his lungs to make sure I've got good placement of the tube."

Maggie took the stethoscope from around Jack's

neck and listened to both lung fields. "Good ventilation. Good tube placement."

"Let's get this show on the road," Jack said. Once everything could be done to stabilize the man, Jack started to relax. "We're going to need to transfer him to the trauma center in Anchorage." He looked at Maggie. "You're next on the list to take a transport. You up for it?"

"Yep. Just need to change into my flight suit and I'll be ready to go," she said. Despite his absent-minded compliment that she was a skillful nurse, remembering his immediate thoughts to the contrary still stung. She had her pride and her nursing skills were at the top of the list. No one would ever again question her skills. Not even Jack.

"That's fine." Jack nodded. "Unless we can get someone else to take the flight."

Maggie stopped him. "Oh, no, I want to go. But I don't want to leave you short-handed here."

"Everyone in the waiting room earlier had minor complaints. I think we can handle it."

"Give me a minute, and I'll be right back," she said to the crew. On her way out of the restroom, Jack stopped her. "I'm sorry."

"I don't have time to chat now, Jack," she said, and walked past him. "Everyone's waiting for me." Re-entering the trauma room, Maggie prepared the patient for the trip, hooking him to the smaller transport machines that fit into the airplane. She worked silently but listened to the conversations of the other staff around her, ignoring Jack's presence at the door.

"We should stay overnight," Kyle suggested. "By

the time we get him there and settled, it will be time
to eat. We could catch a dinner theater. What do you
think, Maggie? Want to see a little of Anchorage while
we're there?"

Maggie finished attaching all of the electrodes to
the patient's chest and flipped on the small transport
monitor. "Sure. Why not?" she said. "I could use a good
time about now."

"Great," Kyle said. "Unless we get called for another
transport right away, we'll be back in the morning."

Jack watched as they closed the ambulance doors and
drove away. Jealousy wasn't an emotion Jack had experienced very often in his life. But now, watching
Maggie plan an overnight trip with another man, even
under the most professional of circumstances, and
watching her drive away with him stirred that feeling.
He had no right to be angry or jealous or anything where
Maggie was concerned.

And he didn't like it one bit. He wasn't even sure he
liked Maggie. And if he did, he couldn't, no, *wouldn't* do
anything about it. Looking down at the wedding band on
his finger, he clenched a fist and shoved it in his pocket.

Knowing Maggie hadn't had time to call Ella, he
called her, knowing she'd worry if Maggie didn't come
home after work.

"Ella? This is Jack."

"Hi, there. Problem at the clinic?"

"No. I just wanted to let you know that Maggie won't
be home tonight."

"My, my, my, Jack. When a pretty girl lands in your
lap, you do move fast," Ella said. Her coarse laughter
scratched down the line.

A muscle in Jack's jaw twitched at the implication. "Ella McGee, shame on you. Get your mind out of the gutter."

"Why? I like it there."

"Maggie's gone on a transport to Anchorage and won't be back until morning. That's why."

"Well, too bad for you," Ella said with a sigh. "I'd rather hear that she was having an evening at home alone with you."

"I don't think so."

"Excuse me, Jack, but you're an idiot if you think Arlene would have wanted you to waste your life."

"Mind your own business."

"You've never told me to do that before—why should I start now?"

"You've never been such a busybody before."

"I'm not the one with my head in the sand," she said.

"Ella! What's wrong with you?"

"What's the matter with you? You've mourned Arlene long enough. It's time for you to get on with your life."

"I am getting on with my life. The clinic—"

"I mean your personal life, and you know it."

"You don't understand—"

"Jack, I do understand. I do. I know what it's like to lose someone and feel like you want to die with them." She took a deep breath and let out a long sigh. "It's time to let her go now. Life is meant to be lived, not watched like some parade passing you by."

Jack paused. "I'll think about it," he said, but doubted he would. Long ago he'd resolved to live alone. It was simpler that way.

"Think about that when you're all alone in bed and wondering why you're cold inside and out." Ella cleared her throat. "Thanks for letting me know about Maggie. I'll talk to you later."

The line went dead. Ella never did waste words. He was sitting there, staring at the phone, when a quick knock at the door roused him. "Come in if you have to," he said.

Amos popped his head through the door. "It's pretty quiet out here, so I'm going to head home unless you need me for anything."

"Can't think of anything," Jack said.

Amos grinned. "Good. My daughter is having her fifth birthday party tonight, and I don't want to be late." Amos started to leave, but hesitated. "If you don't have other plans, you're welcome to come by. Free cake and ice cream."

Jack tried to come up with a reason not to go, but couldn't think of one. Not on a low-gluten diet, or lactose intolerant. "Maybe."

"It's quitting time, Jack. Go home." Amos rapped the door once on his way out and left Jack staring at the door.

Why not? He had to start living sometime. Amos and his family were safe. Suddenly filled with warmth and contentment at attending the little party, Jack locked his office and left the clinic.

Maggie wiped the tears from her face. Laughing, she grabbed a napkin from the table and buried her face into it with a squeal.

Kyle patted her on the back. "You OK, kiddo? What do you think of the Fly By Night Club?"

"I've laughed so much tonight my face hurts," Maggie said, and tried to control the lingering giggles. "Please, tell me it's over. I can't take any more of this," she said.

"Show's over, but the sun's still up and the night is young," Kyle said. "Chilkoot Charlie's, here we come."

"Chilkoot Charlie's? What's that?" Maggie asked as they left the dark interior of the low building for the bright light of early evening. Maggie blinked and reached for her sunglasses. "I'll never get used to this light thing," she said.

"You will. Summer's the easy part. Just wait until winter. Then it gets tough."

"I can hardly wait."

Kyle, Maggie and two other crew members spent the night visiting Chilkoot Charlie's nightclub until the four a.m. closing. From there the small group adjourned to an all-night diner and gorged on giant omelets, gallons of coffee and Alaska chocolate silk pie. On the return flight to Kodiak the medical crew napped, sleeping off the indulgences of the night.

Once home, Maggie let herself into the house and guzzled coffee before dragging herself to the shower. Her thoughts drifted back over the short time she'd been on the island and how the people here had made her feel welcome. An image of Jack lingered as well as the memory of his kiss. Why had he kissed her? Probably all the pent up emotions over the whale. Just needed an outlet. Men didn't react to her with passion. Not really. After her one fiasco in college she'd never been tempted to jump into bed with anyone else. That experience had been a disaster. She'd mistaken his lust for love and had vowed never to do that again. She would never give herself to someone who could make her feel empty and alone. She had closed herself off to the thought of a physical relationship. Until now.

She'd enjoyed the feel, the smell and the taste of Jack. But she was terrified it meant nothing to him. Could she be sure of that? That lone tendril of desire he'd inspired in her wasn't going away like she'd hoped it would.

Over the hiss of the shower she heard the phone ring, but she ignored it, content to let the water soothe her aching body. She hadn't been out all night since college, four years ago. Her body wasn't used to it, and the shower offered some relief. Sleep would be best, but she didn't want to waste an entire day sleeping when she could be out hiking or discovering treasures around the island.

After the shower, Maggie dressed in casual clothes fit to hike, bike or adventure around the island, and returned to the coffee-pot for another infusion of life support.

The flash of the answering-machine light drew her attention, and she pushed the button to listen to the message. Seconds later she clutched the counter, her knees weak at the sound of her father's voice on the machine. She dragged in deep breaths and dropped into one of the kitchen chairs with her head between her knees.

"You'd better not faint," Ella grumbled from beside her.

Maggie turned her head and got a look at Ella's knobbly knees. "Why not?"

"'Cos I'm not picking you up." She sipped at her cup. "Bad back."

Cautiously, Maggie sat up and pressed a trembling hand to her forehead, noticing her skin felt clammy to the touch. "I need to lie down."

"What's got you all knotted up? Oh, there's a message," Ella said and hit the play button on the answering-machine.

Listening to the message the second time wasn't any better than the first. Her father's voice insisted that she return home. Maggie dropped her head between her knees again and groaned. "I can't, I won't."

"Your family got a problem with you living in Alaska?" Ella asked.

"It's not just Alaska." Maggie swallowed. Pain throbbing in her head from an excess of blood forced her to sit upright again. "They just didn't have any idea where I was until now, dammit." Tears clouded her vision, but she blinked them away, determined not to give in to fear, or guilt, or any of those things her father made her feel. She wasn't a little girl any longer. This was her life, and she wasn't going to let him run it or ruin it. Not when she'd finally found a place where she fit in.

"Is there a good reason you don't want your family to know where you are?" Ella asked, and sat beside Maggie, watching her.

"My father has run my life up until a few months ago when I escaped from the asylum that's the family home." She gulped down more coffee. "I just packed up and drove away. Alaska was as far away as I could get and still be in the same country." Maggie met Ella's watchful gaze. "I love my father. I just don't like what he does to me or what he thinks I need to be."

"Don't worry, girl. You're a grown woman now, and you can make your own choices."

Maggie snorted out a derisive laugh, hoping Ella was right but afraid she wasn't. "You don't know my father. He has a way of making the simplest thing seem stupid, and he twists everything until he's right. He's very stubborn."

"You've got new friends here, and I've got a shotgun that packs quite a wallop." Ella laughed, immediately lightening the mood.

Maggie smiled. "That's exactly what he needs," she said, and gripped Ella's hand. "Thank you." Kodiak was going to be her new home. No one, not even her father, was going to take it away from her.

"Why don't you crash on the couch for a while and rest? You look like you could use it." Ella watched as Maggie wandered into the living room.

Maggie dropped onto the couch with a yawn. "I'm sure you're right." Exhaustion had crept up on her. Nothing short of an earthquake could have kept Maggie from falling asleep. The couch was lumpy, but she found a position that suited her and closed her eyes. A nap was all she needed.

Ella pulled a colorful quilt over Maggie. "Whether you know it or not, this is where you belong, honey. I'm gonna help you realize that, or my name ain't Ella McGee."

CHAPTER FIVE

JACK'S pager went off. It was Ella's number and a thrill of anticipation jolted through him at the thought of talking to Maggie again. He hadn't heard from her since she'd returned from the transport, so why would she page him now? An irritable band of guilt hung around his neck when he thought of how they had parted. It had only been yesterday, but already it felt like weeks had passed, and he didn't like it.

"This is Dr.—Jack," he said. "I was paged."

"This is Ella, your fairy godmother."

"What's up, Ella? Cat got a furball again? Dog need its nails cut?" Disappointment escaped in his tone, though he tried to hide it.

"No. It's Maggie."

"She got a furball?"

"No, you twit." Ella hesitated. "Something's wrong with her," she whispered.

Jack jerked upright to attention. "What's wrong with her?"

"I can't wake her up."

Jack relaxed. "She's probably just hung over."

"She's not. Earlier she was dizzy, cold and clammy and almost fainted in the kitchen."

Frowning, Jack tried to imagine what could be wrong as nightmarish thoughts assaulted his brain. Anaphylaxis? Hypoglycemia? A cerebral aneurysm? "Call 911."

"No. She's breathing OK, and I checked her pulse. Can you come over here and look at her before we call in the cavalry?"

"I'll be right there." Jack slammed the phone into its cradle.

Minutes later he burst through Ella's kitchen door, black bag in hand. "Where is she?"

Ella pointed to the living room and backed out of Jack's way.

Jack knelt on the floor and dug a penlight out of his bag. With one hand he pried open one of Maggie's eyes and flashed the light across her pupil, looking for a reaction. It constricted instantly, and he sighed in relief.

"Ow," she said, and scrunched her eyes closed. "What are you doing?" She opened her eyes and glared at him. "Jack? What are you doing here?"

"Ella called me." With expert and gentle hands Jack palpated Maggie's neck, checking for suspicious lumps.

"Why?" She pushed his hands away.

"She said she couldn't wake you."

"Really? I don't think she tried." Maggie started to sit up, and Jack moved back onto his heels as she adjusted her position.

"Are you OK?"

"Yeah. Sure," she said, but her tone was flat.

"Did something happen? Did something go wrong on the flight?" Jack was starting to get worried.

"Nothing went wrong. It was fine."

"Was your date with Kyle OK?"

"My date with…" Maggie stared at Jack and then frowned. "We didn't go on a date. We went on a transport." She stood and swayed, her color ebbing.

Jack eased her back down to the couch before she fell over.

"You don't almost faint for no reason. What's going on, Maggie? Why did Ella call me? She doesn't worry over nothing."

Tears flooded Maggie's eyes, and she covered her face with her hands. "I can't tell you."

"Why not? Did someone hurt you?" he asked, and pulled her close against him. It didn't even cross his mind to be upset that he'd been called away from the clinic for no reason.

"You'll be mad at me if I tell you and send me away," she said, and hiccuped into his shoulder as the tears poured out of her eyes. "I didn't lie to you on purpose. I didn't."

"Tell me," he whispered, her crying lacerating his heart.

"I tried to run away as far as I could. I'm sorry. I can't go back. Don't make me, Jack."

Trepidation settled in Jack's gut like a glob of worms. "What's happened? Who's after you?" He gripped her shoulders and made her face him. He searched her face and cringed at the anguish written there.

"My father," she whispered, as her chin trembled again.

Confused, but relieved it wasn't an ex-husband

hunting her down, Jack relaxed his hold and waited for her to go on.

She pushed a hand through her hair, pulling it back from her face, and met his gaze. "I shouldn't even be telling you this."

"Why not?"

"Because once you asked me if I was running away from something, and I am."

"You can tell me anything. We're friends, aren't we?"

"Are we? Or are we co-workers? Or something else?"

He thought about her question for a moment before he could find an answer that seemed reasonable. "I want to be, if you'll let me. Sometimes I want to be more, but...I can't."

"Can't?" she asked, her gaze searching his for the answer.

"Let's solve one dilemma at a time, shall we?" He smiled and squeezed her hand, offering her some comfort. "Go on with your story."

Unable to hold Jack's gaze, Maggie stared at the floor as she talked. "My father is a controlling, angry man, never happy with anyone or anything. Nothing is ever good enough, especially me. I've always been a disappointment."

"You are not a disappointment," Jack said, his face grim.

Grabbing a tissue from a box on the table, Maggie wiped her face and then proceeded to shred the thing in her hands. She picked up a cushion from the couch and hugged it to her. "According to my father, I'm supposed to return to school immediately, pursue my Ph.D., graduate early and with honors, secure a position teaching at the university level, marry someone worthy of my social status, procreate, and hire adequate caregivers to raise my progeny while I pursue my career."

Jack flopped back against the couch. If it wasn't so serious, it would almost be funny. "What about your wishes?"

"They're irrelevant." She shrugged. "That's why I took off. I've wasted enough of my life following my father's plan and it was time that I made my own path." A deep breath in and a long slow sigh out failed to calm her frayed nerves. "I know I'm still on probation but, please, don't send me away for not telling you the whole story. I'll make it up to you, Jack."

"How did he think he was going to force you into doing what he wants?"

"Oh, he threatened to cut off my finances and all that kind of stuff. I can make my own living, so that really didn't impress me." Maggie stood and paced the room. "I was so careful when I left. I paid off my credit cards. I used cash on the trip up here, and I even took precautions against my nursing license, because it would be simple to trace me through it." She threw the cushion against the wall, wishing it was her father's head.

"So what's wrong with staying here?" Jack asked.

"You don't know my father." She resumed pacing. "He can bully, threaten and browbeat anyone into doing anything, including his children."

"You have siblings?"

"Yes. One brother, James. I call him Jamie just to irritate him." She hugged her arms around her waist.

"How's he dealing with your father?"

"Like a champ. His desires fall in line with my father's wishes, so he never had the challenges I face."

"So, what are you going to do?" Though Jack asked, he wasn't sure he wanted an answer.

"I don't know." Maggie stopped in front of the large picture window that faced the inlet. She watched the ships coming and going, people busy on the docks, and wished she could climb aboard and sail away, never to return. She didn't want to leave, but keeping a step ahead of her father was the only way to hang on to her freedom. Being emotional about it would only hamper her, and give him a chance to turn her away from her wishes.

"What if you just stayed here? What would happen?"

Maggie stared at Jack a full minute, contemplating the possibilities. "I don't know. He'd probably send the company jet for me, expecting me to just get on board and return to Boston."

"You're an excellent nurse, you have a job that you've just started and seem to like. You're an adult woman making your own living, and you've given me a commitment. Why don't you make your stand against your father now? You've got friends you can count on."

Jack approached her from behind and stopped just inches away from her. Tremors still shook her shoulders now and then, the emotion stored inside her muscles twitching in need of release. "Facing your demons is a large part of life and growing up. Why don't you stop running?"

She turned to face him, her blue eyes intense as she held his gaze. "Face *my* demon?"

He nodded.

"Why don't you take your own advice, Doctor?" Maggie asked, and placed her hands on his shoulders. Her gaze dropped to his mouth, and he couldn't move. He knew what she wanted, what she was asking, but he didn't know if he could do it. Without thinking about it, his hands moved to her waist and settled on the inward curve.

The movement stirred her fragrance, and it swirled around him, sinking into his mind. Sandalwood and musk. It was a clean but heady fragrance which stimulated his emotions and his hormones. There must be some sort of pheromone in that combination, because every time he got near her he wanted to touch her and kiss her and forget everything except pouring himself into her. Living in the moment was something he hadn't done in a long time. Something he hadn't even considered until Maggie. But Maggie made him want to change. "Things will turn out OK."

"I don't know. This is new territory for me."

Unable to stop himself, Jack stepped closer to her.

Surprised, Maggie stiffened, but she didn't move away. "What are you doing?"

"I want to kiss you again."

The teasing before a kiss held an intoxicating eroticism, and Jack drew those few seconds out into eternity. Drawing her closer by sheer will, he parted his lips in anticipation of tasting hers, but the scent of her, the texture of her skin and the aura around her held him captive. His head tilted as he watched her eyes close, anticipating his touch, wanting it. Desire for Maggie ripped through him like nothing he'd ever felt before, and he captured her mouth with his.

The first tentative strokes of his tongue against hers broke through any semblance of control he might have at one time possessed. A moan, deep in her throat, told him more than words could have that she wanted this, wanted him. The desperation in her kiss was more than just seeking sanctuary from an emotional upset. She wanted him and his body responded, growing hard from that knowledge and the taste of her.

Unable to control his desire and fearful of what could happen if he didn't, Jack tore his mouth from hers and buried his face in her hair. Trembling from the onslaught of powerful emotions pouring through him, he held Maggie close, needing to hold on to her for support.

"Jack," she whispered. "What are you doing? When you kiss me like that I can't think straight."

"I know. I don't know. Me neither," he said, finally admitting the truth to her, to himself. Pulling back, he searched her eyes and found desire for him unmasked in those incredibly blue eyes.

"What do you think we should do about it?" she asked. There was no guile in her eyes, but they bewitched him just the same.

"We can't really avoid each other, considering we work together," he said. As he'd wanted to do the other evening, he curved his hand around her ear, pushing the hair back from her face.

"Do you want to avoid me?" she asked in a whisper that revealed her vulnerability and tugged at his protective instinct.

He pulled back from her, not sure if he did or didn't. "Not right now I don't. But we have to maintain our professional relationship no matter what else happens between us."

"Agreed." Maggie's eyes curled up at the corners. "Does that mean I can pinch your butt when no one is looking?"

Jack laughed and stepped away from her. The laugh rumbled in his chest and burst from him. He couldn't help it. It felt so good and right to laugh again. Joy threaded its way into every molecule and nerve ending in his body, and he craved the pure happiness it brought him. "No, you cannot pinch my butt."

Jack smiled to himself. Maggie inspired him. *Life was meant to be lived.* But then Ella's poignant words returned to him at that moment. And he knew she was right.

"Maggie, I don't know what you can see in me. I'm not a whole man." The thought sobered his mirth. "You deserve to have someone who can give you everything you want, and I can't." He stroked her cheek as regret stole into his heart, replacing the happiness that had momentarily resided there.

"Why don't you let me decide what I want and what I need?" She stared at him, her playful attitude of a moment ago vanishing. "My father has made that mistake for too many years, and for too many years I've let him. I'm not about to let you jump into his shoes and decide what's best for me either." A tight smile pulled down the corners of her mouth, and the warm look in her eyes grew cold. "What I need is a man who is emotionally available to me and, unfortunately for us both, you're not. I know that. I'm attracted to you, but it's not all I want or need. All my life I've watched my father withhold himself from my mother, and I'm not about to step into that kind of relationship."

Jack followed Maggie to the door. "I'm fine now, Jack. Why don't you head back to work? Your services are needed more there than here now."

CHAPTER SIX

ON SATURDAY, Maggie's first day off since her father's
phone message, she sat at the kitchen table and contemplated the cereal floating in her bowl.

The kitchen door burst open. Maggie jumped to her
feet, knocking over a chair in the process. Ella stood in
the doorway, clutching two bulging bags of groceries.
She rushed to take a grocery bag from Ella, but it
slipped through her hands and dropped to the floor
with a dull thud.

"Hope that didn't have the eggs in it," Ella said, as
Maggie retrieved the bag and placed it carefully on
the counter.

"I'm sorry, Ella. You startled me."

"Startled you?" Ella looked at Maggie's pale face.
"You're jumpy." Ella set her groceries on the counter.
"What's wrong? I know we haven't known each other
for very long, but you can talk to me if you need to."
Ella motioned to the table, and Maggie sat. "It may not
be any of my business, but is this about Jack?"

Maggie nodded and then shook her head. "Yes and
no. It's more about my father's message from the other
day. It's still bugging me. I keep expecting him to walk

through the door and drag me, kicking and screaming, back home."

Ella snorted. "He can try, but he's not going to walk in here without looking down the barrel of my shotgun."

Maggie placed her hand on Ella's. "No one has ever offered to threaten my father before. That's so sweet of you. I really do appreciate it." She sniffed back a tear.

Ella laughed. "You just haven't been in Alaska long enough yet. Did you and Jack talk the other day?"

"Yes. I told him about my situation. My father."

"What did he say?"

"He reminded me that I gave him a commitment."

"That sounds like good advice."

"Coming from a man who can't let go of a commitment and expects me to honor it."

"What do you mean?" Ella asked, her green eyes intense.

"It means that Jack's still deeply connected to his deceased wife." She searched Ella's eyes, but found them unreadable. "I don't mean for that to sound harsh, but I'm attracted to Jack. That's no secret, and he knows it. But I can't let myself become involved with him, even if I wanted to, because he's emotionally unavailable."

"That's the dumbest thing I've ever heard."

"I'm sorry," Maggie said, and dropped her gaze, shamed at her admission.

"Not you. That idiot that calls himself a doctor. Listen. I've known Jack for a long time. Arlene was a wonderful woman, but she wouldn't have approved of Jack's inability to move on with his life."

"How did you know Arlene? Were you friends?"

"The best. She was my daughter."

Tears filled Maggie's eyes as she stared at Ella's face, the miles and years stamped on it. "I'm so sorry. I had no idea." Maggie shook her head and clutched her hands to her stomach as it cramped, feeling like a lump of clay had formed there. "I'm so ashamed. You've had such a devastating loss, and I'm complaining about my family and my social life."

"Don't go getting mushy on me, girl. I loved my daughter and mourned her death. But I let her go. Jack hasn't been able to do it. And he's not been interested in anyone since Arlene died. At least not until you showed up. I've seen the way he looks at you. He's struggling."

"If you want me to find another place to live, I will. Me having a relationship with Jack must be making you uncomfortable." Maggie twisted her fingers together.

"Nonsense. We made a bargain and, like Jack, I expect you to honor it. Unless you aren't happy here and want to go somewhere else."

"No. I love your home. I think of it as my home now, too, and I don't want to leave." Ella had put Maggie at ease and some of her tension waned.

"Good. 'Cos it's too damned hard to find another roommate on such short notice." Ella patted Maggie's hand again.

Relieved laughter bubbled from Maggie at the gesture, and she wiped the sheen of tears from her eyes.

"Enough talk of the past. What do you say we go fishing?" Ella asked.

"Fishing?" Lines from years of exposure to the salty sea air were engraved on Ella's tanned face. If Maggie hadn't known that Ella had fished for a living, she could have guessed.

"Yes. Like out in my boat on the ocean. That's usually where the fish are." Ella rose and started to put away the groceries. "I was planning on going today anyway. Why don't you come along?" She turned and assessed Maggie. "You don't get seasick, do you? 'Cos I'm not holding a bucket for you."

"I don't know. I haven't been in a boat since I was a kid."

"We'll pick up some Dramamine on the way, just in case."

"Great. This should be fun." Maggie helped put the groceries away, then changed her clothes.

An hour later Ella and Maggie unloaded a cooler of sandwiches and drinks from the car. With each woman grasping a handle, they carried the cooler to Ella's fishing boat. The older woman boarded first, and Maggie followed.

"Whew. That thing is heavy. Are you sure we need that much food for just the two of us?" Maggie asked as she flexed her hand, cramped from the weight of the cooler.

"Hello, there."

Maggie turned to find Jack standing behind her. "Jack? What are you doing here?"

"Going fishing." He shot an amused glance at Ella.

"Oh. Did I forget to mention that Jack was coming, too?" Ella asked as she took the wheel and started the engine.

"You might have neglected that tiny detail," Maggie said over the noise and gave her friend a sidelong look. If Jack could take it in his stride, so could she.

"Sorry. Getting old does take its toll on the brain cells. Must have slipped my mind," Ella said with a grin.

"I'll bet. Your mind gets more slippery every year," Jack said, and secured the cooler against the side of the boat with bungee cords.

"This is an obvious surprise. If you don't want me along, I can stay behind," Maggie said to Jack, not sure of how she felt about Ella's matchmaking.

The man couldn't have made her more uncomfortable had he stripped her naked right then and there. The look he threw her left her with little doubt that he wanted her. His gaze always brought a thrill to her that made her heartbeat a little strange, feeling the erratic beat in every cell of her body. But this look turned her knees to jelly and the little spot below her carotid pulse twitched. As if that spot had a memory and wanted Jack's lips on it again.

"You should come along," he said. "It's a great day for fishing."

"You're right," she said, and took a seat behind Ella to hide the quaking of her limbs.

"We're gonna go catch us some halibut. I know a great place," Ella said. "Earn your keep, Jack, and cast off the lines."

With years of expertise pumping through her veins, Ella guided the vessel out of the harbor and into the open sea. Maggie relaxed against the seat cushion and drew in a cleansing breath of fresh sea air. Pretending the wind whisked away all of her cares and problems, she watched the scenery go by. It was exotic in its uniqueness. Rough rock outcroppings the size of football fields thrust out of the sea, plunging upward in search of the sun. Seals dotted the formations in the lower plateaus, barking and bawling. Puffins, black and white diving birds with bright orange beaks, soared over the high spaces. Occasionally one landed here or there to check a nest of young ones or squawk at a rival.

The salt spray soothed Maggie's frayed nerves, and she remembered why she had chosen Alaska, aside from being far from her family. The wildness here spoke to a part of her soul that she had neglected since childhood. Somehow, some way, this land alongside the sea was already the home of her heart, and she knew she couldn't leave it.

"Look there," Ella said, and pointed off the starboard side. "A pod of orcas."

"I wonder how our whale made out," Maggie said. One glance at Jack, and she knew his thoughts ran along the same track as hers. How could they be so in tune, so alike in their thoughts, only having known each other for such a short time? Maggie wondered if something more, something unnamed, had motivated her flight to Alaska. Maybe more than her happiness was at stake.

"The paper reported that it swam off at high tide. It didn't wash up, so F and G believe it made it safely out to sea again," Jack said.

"I'm glad. I hope it made it back to its family safely," Maggie said and watched the pod.

Jack sat across the narrow aisle and watched her. Fewer than three feet separated them, but Maggie felt as if the entire width of the sea loomed between them. Regret burned like an ulcer in her stomach, and she wished for something to cool it. The memory of the kiss they'd shared the other night stole into her mind. Despite the cool air brushing over her skin, the burn of desire flushed her neck and face.

"Here," Jack said, and handed her a bottle of sunscreen. "Put this on. You're starting to turn red already."

Maggie took the bottle, grateful to have something to concentrate on other than Jack's mouth and how well he used it when he wasn't putting his foot in it.

Ella pulled the boat into a protected cove on one side of a rock island. "This is one of my favorite spots. Henry and I used to fish here all the time." She handed Maggie a saltwater fishing rod already rigged and ready to go.

"Was Henry your husband?" Maggie asked, as she tried to throw the baited hook overboard, but only succeeded in tangling the line.

"Yep. He was my man for most of my life." Ella threw her own rig out and settled down with a book to wait. "Met when we were ten. After he died, I never looked at a man the same way."

"Here, let me help you with that," Jack said, and untangled Maggie's line with a skill born of years of experience.

"Thanks. Ella didn't quite tell me what to do with this."

"You just want to drop it over the edge and let it sink. Halibut are flounder, and they linger on the bottom. It's like bringing up a barn door when you hook a big one." Jack tossed the bait overboard and handed Maggie her rod. Their hands bumped as they exchanged the pole. The blush that had started earlier deepened. Maggie refused to look at Jack, afraid that he'd see her emotions written on her face. Desire had no place in her life now. Not for Jack, not for anyone, and she wished it would go away. She remembered her one intimate experience with a man in the past that had hurt her so deeply and ended badly, and this one had disaster written all over it. To open herself up again would take courage she didn't know if she had.

The motion of the boat easing back and forth with the gentle waves lulled Maggie into a complacent mood. She watched Jack as he looked out to sea at a group of seagulls squabbling over some tasty treat they had found. She leaned over the edge of the boat, trying to see beneath the surface.

Jack glanced over to see Maggie looking down into the water. Everything was new and fresh to her, and she smiled as a salmon jumped close to the boat. Joy bubbled from her on a laugh that made Jack smile. Arlene had grown up fishing with Ella, but never went for pleasure. When they had been married she'd said she'd never go again. But now, watching Maggie claim the joy her life had been lacking, his heart cramped a little. He was lucky enough to be there, to share the experience with her, but only from a distance.

"Why didn't you tell me Ella was your mother-in-law?" she asked.

He stole a quick glance at Ella, who seemed to be engrossed in a romance novel and sat with her feet propped up on the rail. "It didn't seem relevant at the time."

"And later?"

"I didn't think it was important, that's all. I wasn't intentionally keeping anything from you."

She nodded, accepting his explanation, and watched as a seagull dove into the water with a splash.

"Does it matter all that much now that you know?"

"No. I don't suppose it does," Maggie said. The tip of his fishing rod moved, and it drew her attention. "Your rod's wiggling," she said.

"My what?"

At his bemused frown she pointed behind him. "Your rod?"

In seconds all three of them had fish on their lines.

"We must have hit a real bunch of them," Ella cried as she rigged up more rods and tossed the baited hooks into the water. "I told you this was a great spot!"

By the end of the day they had hauled in fourteen halibut, varying in size from twenty-five to eighty pounds, not huge by Alaskan standards but definitely keepers.

Exhausted, Maggie flopped like a rag doll in the bottom of the boat, surrounded by fish. "What are we going to do with all this fish? You don't have a freezer big enough to hold it all, do you, Ella?" she asked.

"Jack's got a deep-freeze we can put some in. We can give some to the clinic and sell the rest to a few restaurants in town. They always need fresh fish."

Ella dug out several long fillet knives and handed one to each of them. "Get to work," she said, and grabbed one of the fish to clean.

"We're going to clean them now?" Maggie asked, wide-eyed. "I've never cleaned anything so big in my life."

"Just watch me a few times. You'll get the hang of it," Jack said.

"Says you, who has surgical experience under his belt," Maggie complained with a small pout.

Jack just grinned. They worked together, cleaning the fish. "You want to clean these out at sea. If it's done in the house, you have to be careful. If you don't dispose of the leftovers properly, bears can be drawn to the scent at your house."

"Bears?" Maggie froze, her eyes wide. "Like *real* bears?"

"Yes, real Alaskan brown bears, or Kodiak bears. Remember that patient we had a week or so ago? He'd been cleaning fish at home and before he could remove the skins and leftovers, a Kodiak found him." Jack sighed and handed her another fillet. "Even cleaning up doesn't guarantee that a bear won't be attracted to the scent anyway. They can smell blood and fish from miles away."

"Wow. I had no idea."

"Bears are amazing animals. One of these days you'll see some around town. Before they go to den they will be looking in every Dumpster and back yard for any food they can find."

"From now on I'll be more careful taking out the trash." Maggie laughed.

The trio had had a fun but exhausting day. As they returned to Kodiak, Maggie started to shiver. Though the sun was still high in the evening sky, clouds had moved in, obscuring it, and the air cooled. Jack opened the seat cushion beneath him and pulled out a blanket. "Here, wrap up in this," he said, and handed a green one to Maggie.

"Thanks," she said, enveloping herself in the rough

wool. Jack moved across the aisle, covering the few feet that had separated them earlier, and sat next to Maggie, sharing his warmth with her.

"You did a good job out there," he said, and pulled her close against his side. "You're adapting quickly to the Alaskan lifestyle. Pretty soon you won't ever want to leave."

"I already don't want to leave," she said.

Jack glanced at Ella. Her attention stayed forward as she steered the boat. "Stay," he whispered. He tucked her head under his chin and wrapped his other arm around her.

Maggie sank against his warmth, easing into his side, grateful to share his body heat, and snuggled into the comforting warmth of his body. This was how she'd imagined sharing a relationship with a man. All those memories from the past began to vanish. Jack was healing her. Sharing something as simple as body heat with him felt like a gift, recharging her emotionally. But deep down she knew Jack's inner warmth wasn't available to her. Not now and maybe not ever. Risking her heart on him would just get her hurt. She didn't need that on top of everything else that had gone wrong in her life.

Maybe she wasn't cut out for relationships. Maybe a nice house plant she could talk to and an electric blanket for cold winter nights would be better.

CHAPTER SEVEN

MAGGIE returned to work on Monday to what she was coming to accept as Monday morning mayhem. Anyone who had developed any sort of condition over the weekend landed at the clinic doors bright and early.

People with coughs or summer colds, a weekend warrior who had stepped on a rusty nail, and a mom who had ignored her own fever too long arrived first.

The busier Maggie kept herself, assessing and triaging patients through the clinic, the less time she had to think about Jack and the pain of a relationship with him or the emptiness without him. As the long twelve-hour shift wound down, the staff started to relax around six p.m. The last patient to come through was Tom, the elderly patient who had been at the clinic a week or so ago.

"Hey, there, Tom. How are you today?" Maggie asked as she led him to a treatment room. As they walked side by side, she noted his ashen complexion and sweat-covered face. She grabbed a wheelchair and eased him into it.

"Whew," he said, panting. "That hall gets longer every time I come here," he said as they entered the treatment room.

"Lie down on the gurney and let me put some oxygen on you—that'll help."

For once Tom complied without argument as Maggie assisted him onto the stretcher. Maggie knew he was ill if he didn't have a smart comment to make about his health or the weather.

"Are you having chest pain?" Maggie asked, and placed electrode pads and connected him to the monitor. Adrenaline shot through her system like an Arctic fox after a hare. "Let me call for Jack." She pushed the code-blue alarm button on the wall and staff rushed to the room. When Jack entered the cubicle, he hurried to the side of his friend. Though he examined Tom, he grilled Maggie. "What are his vitals?"

"Pressure's 50 over palp. Sustained V-tach with an uncontrolled rate of 200." Maggie supplied the distressing information. "No chest pain, but he's shocky. I just put oxygen on him, and his saturation is poor at seventy per cent."

"Tom? Can you hear me?" Jack asked, and opened one of Tom's eyelids. "Stay with me, Tom. I need you to stay awake."

Without a word Tom's eyes rolled back, and he lost consciousness. Jack flashed a glance at Maggie and then looked at the monitor. He didn't disagree with her assessment. "We have to shock him out of this," he said, and Maggie handed him the paddles of the defibrillator while she hit the charge button. She was right there, anticipating his needs.

"Charging, 200 joules," she said, and watched the monitor for the signal. "Charged."

Jack placed the paddles on Tom's chest and squeezed

the buttons. Tom twitched. Jack looked at the flat line on the monitor and verified with a carotid check. "Dammit."

Amos started CPR compressions, and Randy gave Tom extra oxygen.

"Again," Jack instructed. A muscle in his jaw twitched.

Seconds later a buzz signaled full charge again.

"Charged," Maggie said in a voice loud enough to be heard over the chaos in the room.

"Again." This time Jack zapped 300 joules of electricity into Tom's chest, praying it was enough to shock the heart out of the lethal rhythm.

"He's got a rhythm now. Junctional, in the thirties," Maggie said, and Jack handed the defibrillator paddles to her. Thinking ahead to what Jack would need, she broke out more equipment, knowing what he'd want in a cardiac emergency.

"Get the external pacer on him and turn it up to eighty." As Jack turned, Maggie placed the pacer pads in his hands.

"Got it."

The silence in the room after the chaos was overwhelming. Everyone in the ER knew and loved Tom. He was a fixture in the community. Watching Jack study the monitor, Maggie could see the tension in his shoulders and the way he clamped his hand on the back of his neck. A muscle in his jaw twitched. She wished she could ease his distress, but she couldn't. None of them could. But together they were doing their best to save Tom.

An hour later, after Tom had been made as stable and

comfortable as possible, they moved him to the mini-ICU. If he survived the night, he would need a pace-maker, which would require a flight to Anchorage.

"Don't you want to send him tonight?" Maggie asked as they left the ICU. "I'll go with him."

"No. It's too risky. I need to call his family in case we can't find a living will. Or in case he doesn't wake up." Hands balled into fists as his sides, Jack paced the hallway outside the ICU. The ICU consisted of a two-room ward converted with extra equipment for the temporary management of critical patients. They either became stable enough to transport after the first twenty-four hours or they died. A dedicated ICU couldn't be justified under those conditions.

"Jack, why don't you go back to your office to rest or go home?" Maggie clasped his sleeve and slowed his frantic pace. Her heart ached for the pain she knew was his. New griefs often brought up old ones and made them fresh again.

"I can't. I've got to stay with Tom. If something happens to him, I'll never forgive myself for not being here."

"Go home for the night," Maggie insisted.

"Watch yourself, Maggie," he said, eyes narrowed. "You don't have the right to speak to me that way."

"I don't have the right? Being a nurse here gives me the right, whether you like it or not. It's my responsibility to remind you of when you're not being rational." Maggie took a deep breath. "Step away from him, give yourself time to settle down, and then go back in. At this rate you'll burn up all of your energy pacing the hallway and won't have anything left if Tom does need you later."

"I need to be left alone." Jack strode away from Maggie and left her standing in the hall alone.

The nerve of the woman. He knew what he needed and it certainly wasn't advice from her. Returning to his office, he was just about to shut the door when Amos walked in.

"How's Tom?" he asked, and dropped into a chair across from the desk.

Jack huffed out a stressed sigh and fell into his own chair.

"He needs an internal defibrillator with a pacemaker, which I can't do here. We've got the external one on him, but that's only a temporary measure at best. If he survives the night we'll fly him to Anchorage tomorrow for pacemaker placement." Rubbing both sides of his head with his hands, he let out a groan. "It's so frustrating that we can't do something as simple as a pacemaker here on the island. If only I had someone who wanted to live here who could run anesthesia. I just can't do it all."

"I'm sorry. I know Tom is a friend of yours, but he knew he needed a pacemaker two years ago. Remember when he came in here almost in the same condition he's in now? He's been living on borrowed time for that long. It was his choice, Jack. And he made it. You can't change that."

A long sigh escaped Jack as he recalled the incident. "Yeah. I know. Doesn't make it any easier to accept."

"Why don't you take off for the night and get some rest?" Amos suggested.

"Why is everyone telling me to go home?" Jack asked, unable to disguise the irritation in his voice.

"Is it because you're as grumpy as a Kodiak bear and look like an old boot?" Amos said, then waved away any response Jack might have made. "I'm sorry, Jack. I can't tell you what to do. But think about it. Take a few hours of rest then come back if you need to check on Tom." Amos left the office and closed the door behind him.

Jack tipped his head back against the leather chair and closed his eyes. Was he out of it? He'd just come back from vacation a few weeks ago, but now it felt like years had gone by since his trip. Rubbing his eyes, he tried to think of what more he could do for Tom.

Nothing. There was nothing he could do other than what he'd already done. But one more check on Tom wouldn't hurt.

With a hand weary from the day's work, Jack pushed open the door of the ICU and walked to Tom's bed. He took Tom's hand and held it. Tom squeezed Jack's hand and struggled to make eye contact. Sedation, fatigue and an ailing heart made it hard for him to focus.

"You look like you're resting OK," Jack said, as Tom struggled to focus on his doctor. Jack turned to the nurse, Gloria. "How's he doing?"

"He's about as stable as we can make him," she said, and double-checked the IV pumps.

"Good." He rubbed the back of his neck. "I'm wondering whether I should spend the night here or go home."

"Go home. We can deal with this guy. There's no reason for you to stay. I've got your pager number, and I'll call if anything changes."

Jack considered Gloria. "I swear there's a conspiracy to get me out of the hospital tonight," he grumbled.

"Hmm. I wonder why?" She pursed her lips and stared at him.

"OK, I give up. I'll go home. If there's any change—"

"I'll call you," she interrupted, and returned to the monitor station. "Promise."

Jack picked up his keys and locked his office. He may as well go home. But to what? An empty house? He didn't even have a dog or a cat to keep him company. His pace slowed as he thought of Maggie. Why not call her, invite her to dinner? She could keep him company for a while. Maybe he could get to know her better. Jack slammed the door of his Jeep and the direction of his thoughts came to a screeching halt.

No, she'd never accept, not after he'd walked away from her in the ICU. He had to remember that they'd been brought together by temporary circumstances and nothing else. He hadn't noticed anything special about her. Nothing at all. Aside from the way her smile made the outer corners of her eyes crinkle up. Or the way her eyes changed color with her moods. And speaking of moods, he'd never noticed how passionate her kisses had been and how they'd stirred feelings and sensations he'd almost forgotten about. But not quite. Remembering stirred something in him he'd thought long dead. Had hoped was long dead. Opening himself again would bring such pain. Not something he wanted ever again.

As Jack opened his front door, he looked around the house, as if seeing it for the first time. The log home was something he'd wanted since the first time he'd seen one years ago. Arlene had loved it from the moment she'd walked into it.

The smile that crossed his lips was brief and full of

sadness. Why did life have to dish out such terrible troubles? As he moved into the living room he picked up a photo of the two of them, taken a few years ago. They'd been on a trip to Hawaii then. So in love it had almost hurt. The pictures on the table progressed in a time line documenting Arlene's illness, her decline and the last picture taken days before her death. She'd changed so much. In the end she hadn't been the person she'd once been. But he'd still loved her. Still did.

Or did he? he wondered as he replaced the picture. Ella had yelled at him more than once to put the photos away, to quit picking at the festered wound in his heart. *Give it time to heal and get on with your life.* Her words still blistered his ears. She hadn't been back to his house since. But he couldn't put them away. Or at least he hadn't been able to at the time. Could he now?

Supper first, though. A man couldn't make decisions with hunger gnawing at him. Thirty minutes later, his appetite sated by a lunch meat sandwich and a bowl of canned soup, Jack brought a cardboard box from the garage. The box was from the last purchase of oil for his Jeep. It seemed disrespectful to be packing away pictures of his dead wife into a box that had been used for engine lubricant. But then again he'd been putting too much emphasis on the stupid things in life. Too much sentimentality. The time had come to start to live again. Without Arlene.

Jack fought back the acid clawing its way up his throat at the thought. He'd need an antacid before this night was over. Again and again, the same thing had happened when he'd tried to put Arlene behind him. He'd felt like he'd dishonored her and what they had meant to each other. Too many people had told him otherwise, and he'd pushed them away. Who was right and who was wrong no longer mattered.

He picked up the last photo and stared at it, seeing the reality of Arlene's death as if for the first time, the last time. In the photo Arlene's hair was thin, damaged by the chemo. Her color was sallow, and she looked like a shadow of herself. Days after the photo had been taken, she'd died. Wrapping the framed picture in last week's newspaper, he placed it in the box on top of the others. He folded the flaps of the box together and taped them shut. Returning to the garage, he placed the box up on a shelf, next to his socket set and wrenches.

As he reached to take the box down again, his pager went off. Dashing back into the house, he grabbed his phone and dialed the hospital.

"What's wrong?" he demanded.

"Tom's gone," Gloria said.

Jack heard the distress and tears in her voice. "What happened? Why didn't you call me sooner, dammit?" Jack dropped into a chair, the angry shot of adrenaline hissing through his system making his knees weak. "Why didn't you call me?" he whispered again.

"It happened too quick, Jack. One minute he was OK, the next he was gone. We tried to code him, but he was just gone. Tom knew it was his time and didn't fight it. You were the last one to see him, and I think he waited for you to say goodbye."

"I'm coming over there." Jack hung up the phone and strode from the house to the Jeep. Within ten minutes he'd parked his vehicle at the front of the hospital and rushed inside.

The ICU was silent. There was no noise in a place that was usually deafening from it. Tom lay in his bed, unmoving, as if just asleep. Jack would have believed that except for the waxy pallor of the man's skin. Seated next to the man on the bed, Jack took Tom's hand. It was still warm. Jack hung his head and shut his eyes.

Gloria came and drew the curtain around them, closing them off from the rest of the unit as Jack said goodbye to his friend.

Maggie didn't know what to do, what to think or how to behave. Jack had kept his distance from everyone at the clinic for two days, and tonight was Tom's funeral service. A small church service at six to be followed by drinks and revelry at Brownies pub.

Not quite what Maggie was used to but, given the relaxed attitude of Alaskans, she wasn't surprised. Tom had been a town leader and exceptional friend to one and all, though he'd never stood out as a wealthy man. He would be missed, but he would be upset if anyone mourned him overly long.

The clinic closed early for the night so that everyone could attend the church service. Maggie wore her best jeans and a light sweater.

For the service Ella wore her finest pair of camouflage pants and a clean white shirt. Hiking boots replaced the fishing boots she usually wore. "You'd better go find Jack," Ella said to her.

"Why do I need to go find Jack? He's a big boy and can handle everything all by himself."

"If he was anyone but Jack you wouldn't hesitate to help or console him. But because he's Jack, you're being stubborn." Ella gave her a nudge toward the back door of the church. "It'll take hours to get out of here. That pastor hasn't seen this many full pews since the last funeral, and he's going to take advantage of it. Go down to the docks and see if Jack's there. That's where he goes when he needs to think." She turned away to wait in line with the rest. "I'll see you at the pub later."

Dismissed, Maggie left the church by the back door. The air was fresh and brisk enough to blow away any lingering sadness from the funeral. She'd only met Tom a few times, but after the service she felt like she knew a little more about him. Maggie enjoyed the short walk to the docks. She leaned against a rail and looked among the boat slips for Jack, but he wasn't there. Bouncing down the set of cement steps to the lower docks, she wondered where he had gotten to.

"What are you doing here?" Jack said from behind her. She almost lost her balance on the edge of the dock. He rose from a bench hidden by the steps. No wonder she hadn't seen him.

"Looking for you. What are you doing?" she asked. Jack started to wander away, and Maggie fell into step beside him.

"I'd say hiding from you, but you'd get mad at me if I did. And it wouldn't really be true."

"I'm glad you didn't say it, then," she said, and shoved her hands into her jeans pockets. "I've been worried about you."

"Why? I'm alive and well." The dullness of his eyes belied that statement.

"I'd say I don't think you are, but you'd just give me some lip about it, wouldn't you?" Maggie elbowed him in a playful way, hoping to jump-start him into having a conversation with her.

"You're probably right. But I wouldn't admit that to anyone." He shrugged and captured her gaze. "Except maybe you."

The wind lured strands of hair out from her tight braid. Loose wisps tickled her face. She reached up to tuck them behind her ear, and Jack captured her hand on its way back down. The gesture surprised her, but pleased her, too. Their pace slowed as they neared the end of the dock. Leaning against the rail, they watched the gentle waves, the boats coming and going with the tide. Maggie sighed, recapturing the contentment that had been lost to her for many years. Loving it here.

"Did you need something?" Jack asked.

She gave a short laugh. "I was just thinking how at home I am here. How right it feels to be standing on this dock in the wilds of Alaska. Kodiak is less cosmopolitan than Boston, but at the same time it feels more like home than home has ever been."

"So you're going to stay after all?" Jack held his shoulders tense.

Her gaze met his, held it, then released it. "I'm staying."

"I'm glad," Jack said, and sighed, his stance visibly relaxing.

"I'm sure Tom's death brings back bad memories of your wife and losing her."

"You're sure?" he asked, and bristled at her words. How many people said such stupid things at funerals? he wondered.

"Yep. I'm sure," she said, and faced him, holding his gaze, challenging him to give back what she was giving him.

With narrowed eyes he stared at her. "How can you be so sure?" Unable to stop himself, he stepped closer and pushed that stubborn lock of hair behind her ear. Again.

"I'm sure, because you're just not yourself."

"How so?" The open honesty in her face humbled him. God, she was beautiful. And she didn't even know it.

"You're withdrawn, short-tempered, and..." She snapped her fingers. "Oh, wait. That's how you *usually* are. I forgot," she said with a silly grin, but then sobered. "If you want to be alone, I'll go."

Those eyes. Surprise and desire sparkled in them. Nothing in the world could make him resist their spell right now. And he didn't want to. For once he didn't want to fight himself. Didn't want to ignore that hint of desire he felt every time he was with Maggie. Right now he wanted to give in and live right in this moment. He felt like that drunk in the ER, hypnotized by her presence.

"You've got a mouth on you, haven't you?" he asked. But he didn't care what came out of that mouth as long as he could press his lips against it and take a long, slow drink.

CHAPTER EIGHT

JACK moved into her, breathing in her unique fragrance of sandalwood and musk. With his hands cupping her face, he raised it to his and kissed her.

Breathless with anticipation, filled with need, Jack opened his mouth over her soft, wet lips and kissed her. Like a dying man, he held on to Maggie, needing her softness, her sweetness. He needed everything she was to keep him from dying right there on the docks.

Maggie parted her lips, opened her mouth to him and drew him to her, hooking her arms around his middle. The ragged breath she drew told him how affected she was. As her tongue tangled and danced with his, he knew he wanted her. Not just in a physical way, though that came raging out from behind the locked door in his heart.

After what seemed like an eternity, Jack pulled back, as breathless as Maggie.

Stunned by the kiss, Maggie searched his eyes. "Why did you do that?"

Unable to hold her gaze, he looked out to sea again, disturbed at how often he found himself desiring intimacy with her. "I don't know. Something comes over me when I'm near you." He sighed and dragged a hand through his hair. "I'm also getting tired of it. Half of the time I don't know what to think or feel when we're together, whether that's at work or in private. I want to touch you, to talk to you, to hear you laugh." He clutched the rail to keep from reaching out and dragging Maggie back into his arms. Each time it was harder to resist her. "Sorry for taking liberties with you. You don't deserve half a man coming on to you all the time. I can't give you what you need or what you want."

"You don't know what I want, Jack. You've never asked me. If you're half a man, it's because you choose to be. For some reason martyrdom is your way of dealing with the world and everyone in it. What happened to you that you'd rather stay alone by choice the rest of your life than take that step to share yourself with someone else?"

"My wife died, that's what happened. How can you ask that? You should be able to understand why I can't reach out." Anger frothed inside him, as if on the edge of a wave ready to crash.

"You do reach out, Jack. You just won't hold on." Maggie turned to walk away from him, but froze. She stared at the steps, where a man stood. He wore casual clothing, and his discomfort in them was obvious. Maggie took a step forward and pressed her hands to her face. Another step closer, then she launched herself at him, laughing and crying and spreading kisses over his face. Jack moved closer, determined to see who had motivated Maggie to spread her hugs and kisses so freely.

"Is it really you? What are you doing here?"

"It's me, little sister." He grinned.

After a boisterous hug, Jamie set Maggie down. "I can't believe you're here," she said. "Just look at you. I haven't seen you in jeans for years. Are you sure you're OK?"

"I can't believe I'm here either. My suits are in the rental car, so have no fear, I haven't gone totally casual on you."

Maggie turned to Jack with a breathtaking smile on her face, and he wished that he'd been the man to put it there. "Jamie, this is Jack Montgomery, my boss and medical director of the clinic where I work. Jack, my brother, Jamie Wellington."

"James," Maggie's brother corrected with a grin in his sister's direction. The men shook hands, but sized each other up as men did who both had some claim on the same woman.

"What are you doing here? Did Father send you?" Maggie asked with a hand clutched to her chest.

Jack detected the uncertainty in her voice. "I'll let the two of you catch up. Maggie, I'll see you another time. Nice to meet you, James," Jack said, and left the siblings alone. His time with Maggie was over for now.

"Yes, Father sent me to bring you back. But while I came this far away from home, I decided to stay for a few days, take some time off."

"You never take time off," Maggie said. "And I'm not going back." Maggie led them away from the dock and back toward town. "Where are you staying?" Jamie always required luxury accommodations wherever he went.

"The Kodiak Lodge was the best I could find."

Maggie nodded. "It's a lovely hotel."

"Yes, it is, and what do you mean, you're not coming back?"

"Exactly that. I've found my place here. For some reason the wilderness and the people here suit me. I've come to love it here much quicker than I ever would have thought. It's as if I was meant to be here, Jamie. I just had to figure out where I belonged in life, and this is it, not back east under Father's thumb."

"If you need to have a little fling, by all means do it, but, please, don't stay in a place like this." He looked around, not seeing the village the same way she did.

"I'm not having a fling," she said, but the heat of a blush filled her cheeks. "I'm staying."

"But Father has everything set up for you."

"Set up for him, you mean."

Jamie shrugged. "Perhaps. But it will further your career if you work with him on this, not against him. He could have you set up for life if you want."

"I can set myself up for life, and I intend to do it here."

"You'd give up your inheritance for this place?" Jamie asked, and looked around with distaste clearly written on his face.

"What's wrong with earning my own money and taking care of myself, instead of depending on someone else to do it for me? Neither you nor Father can take that away from me. I won't let you." Maggie crossed her hands over her chest and huffed out her breath. "I'm his daughter, not his possession. I'll make up my own mind what's right for me, and this is it."

Jamie looked in the direction that Jack had disappeared. "Does the good doctor come with the job? Is that what you're after?"

Maggie stopped and glared at her brother. "What do you mean?"

"I mean, is Jack the reason you're staying?" Blue eyes as clear as her own stared down at her.

"No. Jack's wife died, and he's never going to get involved with anyone."

"That's good. Less incentive for you to stay," Jamie said, and they resumed walking. The Kodiak Lodge was just a few yards away, and they gravitated toward it.

"Jamie, how can you say that? If this is what makes me happy, you should be more supportive of my decision. I'm no longer living the life Father has invented for me."

"Sorry. I've never been good at the mushy stuff. You know me, if there are numbers involved, I'm all over it." He sighed. "Will I be seeing you tomorrow?"

"Not unless you come to the clinic. I work twelve-hour shifts for the next three days, but if you come by around lunchtime I can try to break away to eat with you." Maggie turned and walked home, more determined than ever not to allow the men in her life to change her mind.

Alaskan weather was never predictable and varied as much as the people. Maggie watched out the window of the clinic as her last scheduled shift of the week drew to a close.

"Is it raining?" Catherine asked from behind her.

"Just a drizzle." Maggie turned to her co-worker. Catherine hadn't lost her baby yet, but she was still reluctant to talk about it to anyone other than Maggie. "Why don't you take off, Catherine? I think the weather is keeping everyone home. It's been slow all day, and I can handle the rest of the shift."

Catherine wrapped up the remains of her meal. "If you don't mind, I could use a little extra rest."

"I don't mind at all."

"Let me clear it with Jack first."

"Clear what?" the man in question asked as he entered the empty triage area.

"Is it OK if I go home early? We're pretty slow around here."

"Not any longer. Sorry, but you're going with me. You're next on the flight schedule, and we just received a transport call."

"What kind of transport?" Catherine asked.

"There's an injured man who needs to be flown out of his fish camp. Everyone else is stranded due to the weather, but it hasn't reached us yet. Catherine, you'll be flying with me. Sorry this has come up." He patted her shoulder.

"It's OK. I don't mind," she said, her eyes downcast.

"I need to go to the docks and get the plane ready for the trip. Can you come over to the plane slip in about an hour?"

"Sure. I'll need to get some equipment ready, too."

As soon as Jack had left, Catherine burst into tears. Without hesitation, Maggie pulled the woman into her arms and hugged her tight. "Shh. Don't worry, honey. You don't have to go."

"You heard Jack. It's my turn. We always rotate to make it fair to the staff, but I don't want to go. The flight could cause a miscarriage, and I'm almost through the most dangerous time with this one." Catherine sniffed and pulled back, trying to wipe away the moisture that flooded her eyes. "No. I'll go. It's just a transport, right? I'm sure it will be no big deal." The anguish in her eyes betrayed her words.

"It'll be OK. You'll see. Let's get that equipment together, and I'll help carry it."

Jack proceeded with the maintenance check of the medical transport float plane. The community had raised money and with the help of a private endowment had purchased it for the clinic. As a licensed pilot, Jack flew most of the local transports. He'd been flying in the turbulent and dangerous air over Alaska for ten years without mishap. He had no reason to believe this trip would be any different. Just as he completed the maintenance check footsteps on the dock alerted him to Catherine's arrival. "Catherine, I'll be right with you. We'll get going in a few minutes." Dragging himself out of the internal storage compartment, Jack stepped out onto the float. The welcoming smile faded from his lips.

Maggie stood on the dock, dressed in her flight suit, her arms filled with gear.

"What are you doing here?" he asked, confusion written on his face. "Where's Catherine?"

Maggie smiled and gnawed her lip. "Catherine and I switched places. She's going to work out the end of my shift, and I'll take her flight."

"Why?"

"I haven't taken enough flights since I've been here

to keep me happy, so we traded. It's no big deal, Jack." Maggie handed him equipment to stow. There would be enough room for the equipment, one patient on the stretcher, the nurse and pilot, and a small cooler of food, but nothing else. Every other speck of space was filled. Some of the equipment was permanent, built into the plane for monitoring patients and storage of supplies.

They finished loading the plane before Jack spoke again. "You should have let me know about the switch."

"You left the clinic too fast. Is it a problem to do the transport with me?"

"No," he said, but his eyes were wary and his jaw clenched.

"If you have difficulty working with me, Jack, you need to tell me. We can be professional about this, can't we?"

"We can. And we will." Dammit. Why did Maggie have to be the one to go with him? Life had been much simpler before Maggie Wellington had burst into his clinic and his life.

As Jack taxied the plane away from the dock, he watched for other airplanes and boat traffic and maneuvered the plane safely through. Maggie adjusted the headset so it fit her. It was the only way they could communicate during the flight. The engine was too loud for casual conversation.

"Are you receiving me?" he asked, and spared a quick glance in her direction.

"Yes." Maggie nodded. "Where is the camp?"

"About an hour away, if the weather holds."

"Think you can put up with me that long?" Maggie asked.

Jack turned to face her and that grin of hers.

"I can deal with you that long. How's your brother doing?"

"Oh, he's having more fun playing the stock market on the computer than coming out of the hotel." Maggie shook her head and sighed. "I've tried to get him to do some tours, but he won't budge. The market must be hot now."

"What does he do for a living? Even in casual clothing he looks like a money man."

"You're right. He buys struggling companies, chops them into pieces and sells them for profit. Not something I understand, in more than one way."

"Me neither." The engine whined. The speed of the plane forced Maggie back into her seat and she was thankful for the doorhandle to hold on to. After they were airborne they picked up their conversation.

"We're in the putting-things-back-together business, aren't we? I mean, people come in torn apart by a car accident or a bear or disease, and we try our best to keep them whole or make them whole again."

Jack considered her words and felt himself relax, intrigued that she could so easily read his thoughts, share his philosophy. In some ways Maggie had been born to be here in Alaska with him. She matched the vivid beautiful landscape. She didn't just agree with him because it was easy. They shared the same ideas, the same philosophy. Loving her would be easy for the right man. It just couldn't be him. "That's what we do. And you're very good at it. I haven't had much chance lately to let you know I've really appreciated your skills in the clinic. All I've heard is Maggie this and Maggie that, and how good Maggie is. You're not only good with tasks and anticipating what I need in a crisis, you're great with people, making them feel comfortable in situations that are out of their control."

"You're going to make me blush, Jack."

"Sorry," he said, and looked to see if it was true.

"Don't be sorry, keep it up. I like it."

Jack laughed, surprised at how good it felt to laugh with her. "Don't push your luck, Wellington. You're going to work for any compliments you get from me."

The giggle that escaped from her mouth crept into his ears and stayed there for him to remember.

As they approached the fish camp, they followed the river to the designated area. Thankfully Jack was familiar with the camps along the river. When he brought the plane down toward the surface of the river, Maggie gripped the instrument panel and clenched her eyes shut.

"Don't worry," Jack said with a laugh in her ear. "We're on floats. We won't sink."

"I hope you're right," she said, her voice a tight squeak. "This is my first float-plane landing."

"Any landing you can walk away from is a good one," he said as he taxied the plane to the dock of the remote cabin. A lone figure stood on the dock and waved to them.

"Dammit. That guy doesn't look hurt. If we've flown in here for a hangnail, I'm not going to be happy."

"Let's take a look and see before making judgments." Maggie patted him on the knee, and Jack's spurt of anger fizzled down to irritation. She was right again.

They got out and secured the plane to the floating dock. The boy waiting was a young teen and not the victim described by the rescue team. "Are you injured?" Jack asked.

"No, it's my grandfather," the boy said.

"Why don't you take us to him?" Jack asked, and shouldered one of the medical bags that Maggie handed to him. They looked at each other with identical concern.

No one had told them about a second person.

"What's your name?" Maggie asked.

"Abel Topsekok," he supplied as they hurried toward a small cabin. No trees grew in the area, but grasses grew in wild clumps, clinging to the ground with tenacious roots. Low bush plants were loaded with berries not yet ripe enough to be picked. Bears in the area would soon be after them.

Abel opened the door and led them to the cot where his grandfather lay on his side, covered by a heap of blankets.

Abel spoke to the man in a language that neither Jack nor Maggie understood.

The injured man opened his eyes and looked at Jack, nodded and closed his eyes again.

"Let me get some vitals on him," Maggie said, and placed a blood-pressure cuff on the patient's left arm.

"Abel, does your grandfather understand any English?" Jack asked as he took in the ample size of the patient. Though not tall, he was stout in the middle, likely from a traditional native diet, high in fat, required to survive the vicious winters in remote Alaska.

"Very little. He's a traditional man and has lived in

his village all of his life. He always said there was no reason for him to learn English when he had no reason to leave his village."

"I see." Jack knelt beside the bed and examined the gunshot wound on the man's left side. "How did this happen?"

"I tripped, and my gun went off." Abel bent his head and wiped his face on his shoulder. "I was hunting for rabbits," Abel said, tears choking his voice. "Is he bad?"

"Bad enough. He's going to need surgery for sure. Tell him we need his permission to take him to the clinic in Kodiak. And ask him if he has any allergies."

Abel and his grandfather exchanged a few sentences, and the patient nodded. "OK," he said with great effort.

"What's your grandfather's name?" Maggie asked.

"Elmer Topsekok," Abel said, and held on to his grandfather's hand.

"We should probably give him a little morphine to take the edge off of his pain," Maggie said.

"Go ahead. Two milligrams as soon as you get an IV hooked up." Maggie and Jack worked together. They packed the wound with gauze soaked in Betadine solution to prevent infection, started an IV for hydration, and made Elmer as comfortable and stable as possible without over-sedating him with morphine.

"Let's try to sit him up now," Jack said, and slid his arm behind the man's shoulders.

It took all three of them to get Elmer to his feet. Dizzy from loss of blood, he swayed and paled. "You're going to have to walk to the plane," Jack said. "We can't carry you."

Abel translated and pointed to the plane. Elmer

nodded and shuffled along, clutching his injured side, flanked by Maggie and Jack. Though it took only minutes for the awkward group to get to the plane, to Maggie it felt like hours. So many things could go wrong. She was just grateful that Jack was with her. They had to work together to save this man's life. "Once we get you inside you can lie down on the stretcher," Maggie said. Again, Abel translated.

"You realize that Abel's going to have to go along, don't you?" Maggie whispered to Jack.

"I know." A muscle in his jaw twitched. "We can try to squeeze him into a corner, but we'll be over the safe weight limit." Jack glanced at the men as they climbed into the plane. "Elmer looks like a solid guy and so does Abel."

Lightning split the sky and thunder echoed, still miles away. Despite the cool weather, Maggie started to sweat. But she climbed into the plane. She hooked up a blood transfusion to Elmer. His color had almost turned green during the walk to the plane, and the effort it had cost him to get into the plane was enormous. Blood seeped through the bandage they had applied against his wound. Maggie reinforced the dressing with more gauze padding. Removing it could start the blood flowing faster, so she left the original in place.

During the time it had taken them to stabilize Elmer, the storm that had kept the other planes grounded worked its way toward them, threatening, closer and harsher, just a few miles away now. Jack looked at the sky boiling with black clouds and slashed with lightning. "We'd better get moving."

They loaded the equipment and stowed it in the rear of the plane.

"How are we going to do this?" Maggie asked. Worry like she'd never known seared through her and burned like a hot coal in her gut.

"I don't know. We're going to be seriously over-weight with all of us in the plane," Jack said, his jaw aching. "We're not prepared for this. There's nothing else I can leave behind." He stood on the plane's float. Maggie stood on the dock.

"Leave me behind," she said, as a few fat drops of rain hit her in the face. As she looked overhead at the storm, something inside Maggie fused. Resolve, strength and courage mixed together, and she knew she could do it. She could remain behind without fear, and she took a step backward. "You'd better get going before that storm breaks and we're all stranded. Elmer won't tolerate much more blood loss. You can come back for me when the storm lets up." Her brave words ended when her voice cracked.

Jack leaped onto the dock beside Maggie and grabbed her arms, pulling her close. "This is not accept-able, Maggie. I can't leave you behind. *I won't*. You're not prepared to stay out here. This is real wilderness, not some pretend camp-out in the back yard."

"There's the camp that the men used. It's not the Ritz, but I'll be safe in it. And you'll come back for me as soon as the storm lets up, right?" She hoped that Jack couldn't feel the trembling vibrations in her limbs, the anxiety that shot through her system. "It'll be OK, Jack. I trust you. I trust you." She reached out and pressed her palm to his cheek, wanting to touch him again, feel his strength and bring some of it into her.

Jack huffed out a sigh of exasperation and raked his

hand through his hair. "How can you say that? This isn't an issue of trust, Maggie. You're safety is important to me, and I'm responsible—"

"Then be responsible and take the patient in." She blinked, breaking the intensity of his stare. "Then come back for me."

Jack dragged her into his arms and held on to her like he'd never let her go. A tremor rocked him and resonated through her. "I don't want to leave you behind. I can't."

"You have no choice, Jack. Elmer is in a critical condition and getting worse by the minute. He needs more medical attention than we can give him out here. Keep your focus where it belongs. Don't go getting emotional now." She pulled back and clutched his hands, searched his eyes. "This is what we do, remember? We fix things, broken people. Get into that plane, and go fix him."

"Maybe I can do some surgery in the cabin—"

"And use what for anesthesia? Two milligrams of morphine? Be realistic, Jack! I'm sure the worst thing that will happen to me is being bored. I have my jacket. We have a cooler of food I can keep, and I'll be fine," she insisted, hoping it was true. She had to be strong for him. And for herself. "I'll be…fine." Her voice cracked, and she swallowed the lump in her throat.

"God, Maggie. This isn't right. I don't want to leave you." Jack looked at her beautiful face, the intensity of her blue eyes, memorizing every nuance of her. Planting a desperate kiss on Maggie's trembling mouth, Jack clung to her, tasted her, desired her. Despite the tense situation, Jack kept his lips pressed to hers. Every second his lips moved over Maggie's was a second seared into his memory. But he needed to imprint her feel, her taste, her everything onto his soul. "I'll be back as soon as I can."

"Don't take any chances you don't have to," she said. "Be safe."

Jack stepped away from Maggie. "I'll be back," he said, but kept his eyes on Maggie as if seeing her for the first time.

Or the last.

He climbed into the plane and took his seat. Abel took Maggie's seat.

"Be safe, Jack," she said, and memorized his face. She reached her hand out, and he squeezed it.

"I'll come back for you," he said, reinforcing his commitment to her.

"I'll be waiting."

"It could be two days until the storm lets up enough for me to fly in again," he said. "It's a bad one."

Maggie could hear regret choking his voice as he shoved his headset on, and her throat closed, preventing her from responding to him. She nodded and withdrew from the plane.

Jack closed the door. The engine started and the propeller hesitated once, then spun as the motor caught. Maggie looked through the windshield at Jack. Grimfaced, he gave her a thumbs-up.

Maggie returned the gesture and watched as the plane taxied out into the swollen and choppy river. The plane bobbled over the waves, trying to pick up enough speed to take off, and Maggie held her breath, her heart thrumming in time with the prop. Soon, they were safely in the air. Jack banked the plane and flew over her, tipping the wings in both directions in final salute.

Rain now fell in a steady downpour, but Maggie stood on the dock until the plane had disappeared. She wiped away the rain mixed with tears from her face. She picked up the cooler from the dock and walked up the muddy path to the camp.

Once inside the small cabin, she set the cooler on the dirt floor and shrugged out of her wet coat. A dust-covered kerosene lantern sat in a corner. Obviously it wasn't used very much. Maggie looked around for another light source. A similar lantern with battery power sat in the center of a picnic table. A twist of the knob verified that the lantern was in usable order and she set it in the middle of the table.

Then the storm erupted with blinding lightning and deafening thunder. Maggie sat at the table with her hands folded up, praying that Jack had made it back before the worst of the storm hit.

Jack landed the plane in the inlet and slowly released his clenched, numb fingers from the wheel. If the transport had taken any longer he'd have lost the feeling in both hands. The ambulance crew waited on the dock. As soon as he cut the engine, the men moved to open the door of the plane.

"Is my grandfather going to be OK?" Abel asked.

Jack heard the crack of his voice, but didn't know if it was from emotion for his grandfather or fear of the storm. "We're going to do everything we can to make him better. After you're settled at the hospital, we'll try to contact your family in your village."

"My grandmother will want to hear from us by tomorrow."

"She'll be worried if she doesn't hear from you?" Jack asked.

"She'll be furious!" Abel exclaimed. "We're supposed to bring back fish for her to dry for the winter. If she doesn't get started now, they won't have enough to last."

"Your grandfather won't be ready to make the trip back to the village by then, and certainly won't be able to fish. But we'll make sure your family has enough food for the winter."

Only two hours had passed since Jack had returned to Kodiak, but it felt like two days. Getting the patient to the clinic and stable wasn't the problem. Waiting out the storm was killing him. To keep busy and be ready to take off when the storm let up, Jack filled the plane with food, his rifle, extra ammo, sleeping bags and other survival gear.

Lightning shattered the sky as the storm poured its worst down onto the island. After adjusting the radio to the weather channel, Jack listened to the forecast, hoping he would hear some good news. Another storm was coming on the heels of this one, but in between he might catch a break.

An unexpected knock on the door of the plane interrupted the weather report. Ella and James stood outside, wearing bright orange ponchos. Jack opened the door. "What are you two doing here?" he shouted.

"Are you going back for Maggie?" Ella yelled back.

"Yes."

"It's too dangerous for you to fly right now. You know that," Ella said. "Don't be an idiot, Jack. She's safe for a while, isn't she?"

"I can't leave her out there by herself," Jack said. Ella would understand why he had to go, why he needed to go. "I can't leave her."

"Bring my sister back. She's not up to this kind of situation. Nothing like this has ever happened to her before," James said, adding to the burden of guilt already weighing down Jack's heart.

"Nothing like this has ever happened to me either," Jack said. He slammed the door against the rain, wishing he could shut out his feelings as easily, but the rain continued, as did the trembling in his heart. Ella and James dashed away to the safety of the pub beside the dock.

Jack's hands clenched into fists, and he held them to his head, indecision clawing at his gut. Was he pushing himself beyond his abilities by going back into the storm for Maggie? He watched overhead as lightning dissected the sky in jagged flashes, like the wrath of some angry god.

Storms this severe weren't unusual in Alaska, and he'd braved many over the years, but he'd never intentionally flown into one. Jack pulled the hood of his jacket up over his head and got out of the plane. He entered the pub to wait with Ella and James. Maggie was safe at the camp for the moment. Killing himself to get back to her wouldn't help any of them. But it was killing him not to go.

Maggie ate a sandwich and drank a can of soda. The damp air seeped into her bones, chilling her. She moved to the bed. It was more like a wide cot, but it worked. When she sat down, the fragrance of dried grasses and herbs wafted around her and soothed her frayed nerves. Huddled against the wall with a blanket thrown over her lap, she tried to stay warm. Her thoughts, more than anything else, were the coldest part of her.

What if Jack didn't make it back? No one would know where she was. Would they? Would someone else come to rescue her? Could James organize a rescue mission? Ella would. Maggie's tension eased a bit at that thought. Ella could compete with the storm overhead for attention.

But as she thought of the danger Jack was going through to save that patient, a sheen of moisture blurred her vision. Bravery gave way to emotional exhaustion. She flopped onto the bed and fell into a restless, dream-filled sleep.

She dreamed of Jack and how strong he was. Bravery and courage were hard to come by these days and Jack had a strong dose of both. Sometime later she woke with a dreamy laugh as the Jack in her dream shook his jacket out and sprayed her with rainwater. In her dream she wiped away the moisture from her face.

But the water dripping on her face was real and it woke her fully. Blinking sleep and the dream away, she didn't know what she would do about a leaky roof. She just hoped it wouldn't collapse.

When she climbed from the bed, Jack stood beside it, and he was no dream.

"Oh, Jack! You're back!" she cried and flung herself into his arms.

Cold and wet, the man looked like he'd jumped into

the river fully clothed. But she didn't care. With a handful of his collar, she jerked his face down to hers and kissed him.

Jack had never tasted anything as precious as the kiss Maggie planted on him. Urgency drove him, and he plundered her mouth with his tongue, her warmth infusing him with a heat he'd all but forgotten. The relief that poured out of him was almost tangible, and he quivered. Maybe it was from nerves shot from the long day he'd had flying through the storm. Or maybe the rain had given him a chill. Or maybe it was just from having Maggie in his arms where he wanted her that fed the need pulsing through him.

With a gasp Maggie pulled away and framed his face with her hands. "I'm so glad to see you," she said, and her bottom lip quivered.

He stroked her mouth with his thumb and cupped the back of her head, bringing her close again for a hard, quick kiss. "I was going nuts. I had to come back. Thinking about you out here alone in the wilderness and this storm was more than I could take."

"You put yourself in danger for me. No one has ever done that. I've never been worth that to anyone." Tears welled in her eyes.

"You're worth it to me," Jack said, and took her mouth with his. Her muffled cry made him want to rip her clothing from her and make love to her right then and there. Knowing she wanted him filled him with power. He felt like a man again. She'd made him a man again.

"Maggie," he said, not knowing what to say or how to say it. But he needed her with every cell in his body.

"Take your coat off," she whispered, and helped him remove it.

"I'm probably getting you all wet. I'm sorry." Jack hung the coat on a peg by the door to dry and tried to quell the desire throbbing through him.

"I couldn't care less about the water. I just want to be held by you."

The look of need and desire in Maggie's eyes left him with no doubt that she wanted him.

"You shouldn't have come back until the storm eased," she said and stepped toward him.

As he stepped closer to her he removed the heavy cotton shirt that covered his T-shirt and dropped it on the table. "Come here," he said, and opened his arms.

CHAPTER NINE

MAGGIE eased into Jack's arms, and they clung together for a long time, drawing comfort and strength from each other. "I can't believe you're back, but I'm so glad you're here," Maggie said. Realizing he was shivering in her arms, she pulled back from him. "Did you bring more clothes? You're soaked."

"They're in the plane," he said, and pulled the slicker over his head. "I'll go get the supplies I brought and be right back."

When he'd left, Maggie dropped into one of the chairs, rocking back and forth with excitement, fear and overwhelming desire for him. Oh, God, how was she going to get through this night without flinging herself into Jack's arms? Oh, right. She'd done that already. Not that he'd seemed to mind, but they were supposed to be keeping it professional between them.

Minutes later Jack returned and dumped an armload of supplies just inside the door. "There's more to come," he said, and disappeared back into the rain.

Maggie watched for his return and opened the door for him. While Jack dealt with the survival gear, Maggie moved the food into the kitchen area. He spread a sleeping bag onto the first bed and tossed a bag onto the second one.

"How is Mr. Topsekok?" Maggie asked, as she watched Jack open the sleeping bags. She tried not to wonder if they would zip together into one.

"Much better. Giving him the transfusion when we did helped a lot. It's a good thing we took Abel with us, too," Jack said, and propped the rifle beside the door.

"Why is that?"

"He's diabetic and had a hypoglycemic episode."

"Is he OK now?" Maggie asked, relieved they hadn't left him behind.

"He's fine. Gave him some dextrose IV and took him to the diner. The kid ate like a horse." Jack laughed.

"I'm glad they're going to be OK." Maggie smiled, more at ease now that they were on a safe subject. "You did the right thing."

Jack ran a hand through his rain-soaked hair, shoving it back. He dug a towel out of a duffel bag. "I've been on such an adrenaline kick since I left here, I'm not sure I'll be able to sleep." He held out a hand that visibly quivered.

Maggie took the towel from his hands and directed him into one of the chairs. "Sit."

"Why?" he asked, but sat.

Maggie ignored the question and dried his hair with the hand towel. She rubbed his thick hair, squeezing excess moisture from it. With fingers that shook a little she fluffed the strands into order and draped the towel over his shoulder. "Why don't you change into dry clothes and try to relax?"

Maggie moved away as he opened a duffel bag of

clothing. With her back to Jack, she tried not to picture what he looked like.

Naked.

"Can you give me some help?" Jack said.

She heard him struggling with the clothing. "What kind of help?"

"My boots. They're stuck."

Maggie turned, and her mouth went dry. With no ability to control her hungry gaze, she took in Jack's state of undress all at once. Dark hair scattered over his bare chest and converged into a line that dropped low over his flat abdomen. The muscles of his chest outlined his anatomy better than any textbook could ever hope to illustrate. Lean but well defined, Jack stood and waited. His eyes were half-closed, and she couldn't read his expression.

Clamping down on her overcharged hormones, she knelt beside him and unlaced one of the heavy boots he wore. The water inside created suction that she worked hard to release. With a slurp it gave way and Maggie almost landed on her butt as it came off in her hands. After she'd removed the second boot, she moved away, afraid she'd betray the need that welled within her.

Emotionally available or not, she wanted Jack with her heart and her soul. She wanted to touch him, hold him, feel his skin beneath her fingers and against her, inside her. She thought back to her brother's words about having a fling. Could she do that with Jack? Could she open up to him when she knew he couldn't do the same for her? Could she just have sex with him and leave it at that? All her life she'd obeyed the rules and done what had been expected of her. When was she ever going to do something for herself? After that first disastrous relationship in college, she'd never been intimate with a man again. But Jack made her feel things that she shouldn't be feeling. Her heart pulsed, her mouth went dry and other parts of her ached for him.

Listening, she heard Jack remove the remainder of his clothing and the light rustle of dry fabric as he dressed again.

"You can turn around now. I'm dressed."

"OK." She turned, but didn't look at him, just fiddled with looking through the supplies. "You brought enough stuff to keep us going for a while," she said, amazed at how much he had brought.

"I didn't know how long we'd be here, so I brought plenty." He handed a backpack to her. "Ella sent some things for you."

Maggie took the bag and rummaged through it. She brought out a pair of sweatpants and shirt. "That woman is a gem," she said, and hugged the fresh clothing to her. A toothbrush and toothpaste, brush and a hair tie, socks and clean underwear. Maggie stepped to the sink and brushed her teeth, savoring the fresh clean taste.

"I'm going to try to sleep a while. It's been a long day. Goodnight, Maggie," Jack said, when she'd finished.

"Goodnight." Even though Maggie had just brushed her teeth, her mouth went dry at the thought of sleeping next to Jack. "Which bed do you want?"

"Doesn't matter," Jack said with a shrug.

"Why don't I keep the one I had, and you take the other?" she asked.

"Fine," he said, but didn't move away. He just stood there and stared at Maggie.

"What? Do I have toothpaste on my face or something?" she asked, and started to wipe her mouth.

Jack grabbed her arm before she could complete the motion.

"No. Don't do that."

Before she could think or act, Jack stepped up to her and took her mouth with his. Her breath caught in surprise. Opening her mouth to his, she welcomed the soft warmth of his tongue, satisfied by the touch, the intimacy of kissing him, and she met him stroke for stroke. Strong arms moved around her waist and pulled her tight against him. The fabric of his pants was no barrier and left her with little doubt that Jack desired her. At least physically. The dampness of his hair beneath her fingers reminded her of the storm outside. But it was nothing compared to the storm raging inside her.

Jagged bolts of desire, want and need shot through her. Beats of thunder from her heart echoed in her soul, and she knew it would never be just sex with Jack.

Jack released her lips and pressed his forehead against hers, his breath coming in quick gasps. "I want to look at you."

Maggie's hands moved to the buttons on her shirt, but then fear stopped them. Her lips clung to him, but otherwise she couldn't move.

Jack covered her hands with his, and they trembled as he released the first button on her shirt, and the second, and the third. "You are beautiful," he said as he pushed aside the fabric that kept her skin from his view. Maggie tipped her head back and he pressed his lips to her collar-bone, tasting the tender flesh there. She was as soft as she looked, and he traced the tip of his tongue upward, past the dip at the base of her neck and stopped to outline her ear. Her breath came in uneven shudders, as did his. Nibbling on the lobe of her ear, he knew he couldn't stop himself from exploring every inch of her body.

He felt like a drunk, and Maggie was his drink. "I need you, Maggie," he whispered in her ear. "I want to make love with you so badly it hurts," he said. The words sounded strange, forming in his brain. "I know I shouldn't want you the way I do, but I can't stop myself. Tomorrow I may hate myself, but tonight I'll hate myself more if I don't hold you." His hands traced the edges of the lace bra molded to her curves, and he was lost to her. "Will you let me?"

She looked up at him with her vulnerable big blue eyes. "I've only been with one man," she said softly, pausing to gauge his reaction. Her eyes were full of pain, full of remembered sorrow. "And it was a disaster. It devastated me." Jack stroked his hand down her face, brushing away her silent tears. Maggie looked deep into his eyes, offering herself to him. For the first time laying herself bare. "I want you to take away that old memory and give me a new one to keep with me," she whispered. "Make me forget, Jack. Please."

Jack sought her mouth with his and Maggie gave in to a kiss full of longing, regret, passion and need. She wanted him, she wanted this to go on for ever.

Jack dropped hot, open-mouthed kisses on her face and her neck and her ears as his hands cupped her head. He wanted to erase any bad memories from her past. He wanted to give her the experience she deserved. To show her how perfect this could be. Tunneling his hands into her hair, he held her close. He felt her tentatively brush his skin with her hands. Fingertips went up his spine to his neck, urged his arms up, and he tore off his shirt.

With his mouth on hers, he led her to the cot and laid her down on it, then covered her body with his, needing to touch every inch of her, breathe in her fragrance and keep it in his mind forever. A woman's curves and softness had never been as welcoming as hers were right now.

Licking and kissing her neck and moving downward, Jack sought out the lush fullness of her breasts with his mouth, following the contours and curves. His fingers dragged down the straps of her bra and moved to the back and released the clasp.

He clamped his mouth onto a rosy nipple and sucked it, flicking the tip of his tongue across the smooth skin until it puckered.

Maggie twisted, pressing more fully into him, and her hands gripped his arms, giving him unobstructed access to her breasts. "Jack," she sighed. "Oh, Jack." He reached for her other breast and filled his hands with her. Unable to resist, he licked the other soft, pink peak and watched as it responded to his touch.

Maggie's hands got busy. They roamed over his shoulders and arms and raked through his hair. Each touch, each breath, each sigh made him want her more.

Jack stripped off his jogging pants, but then sat on the edge of the bed, clutching the mattress in his hands. He hesitated, hating himself for wanting Maggie, disregarding his vows, until she knelt behind him. The feel of her breasts pressed against his back and her arms around his neck felt so right. So very right. But how could he make love with her?

How could he not?

"Let's take this slow, Jack. There's no reason to rush," she said, and held on to him, rocking him, the tips of her breasts teasing the skin on his back. He turned and looked at her.

Maggie's blue eyes were dewy with desire. Her hair, mussed from his hands, escaped its braid. Lips, swollen from his kisses, parted with her breathing.

"Sit back," he said, and Maggie moved back onto her heels. Jack turned toward her, and his glance roamed over her breasts, their fullness beckoning him to touch them again. With one finger he drew an imaginary line from her jaw, down her neck, over the bump of her collar-bone and lower until the curve of her breast interrupted the line. Turning his hand, he cupped her breast, then reached out for the other.

"Maggie," he whispered, and captured her gaze, trying to see into her soul. "I need you like I've never needed anyone in my life."

"I need you, too," she said. "If all you can give me is this one night, I'll take it." She drew him to her, then lay back on the bed. Jack's hands worked the fastening of her jeans and dragged them off her hips.

Now they were flesh to flesh, and Jack plundered her mouth, unable to get enough of the taste and the feel of her, wanting to crawl inside her. Tangled together like this, Jack couldn't think of anything else, except being with her. No past, no present, no future. Wanting to explore more of her body, his hand moved downward over the curve of her waist and hip to her soft woman's flesh. Delving inside, he almost lost control as he found how ready she was for him. "Maggie," he whispered, unable to create any other sensible thought.

"Come here," she said, and guided his body to hers and sought his mouth.

Hesitating at the edge of joining with her, a flash of sanity struck him. "I don't want to make you pregnant."

"I'm on the Pill for other reasons. I need you now."

Jack eased inside her moist flesh.

And almost exploded as her tender flesh gripped his. He grabbed her hips and gasped. "Don't move."

"What's wrong?" she asked, but stilled.

"Nothing. It's just been a long time for me, and I want to please you."

He blew out a breath, trying to control his body. But she felt so good and so right to him. Jack moved his hands up to cup her face and gave her a long, slow kiss, hoping to distract himself from how he slid so easily into her and how her body accepted him, how perfectly they fit together. Maggie drew her legs up, wrapped them around his hips, and he was gone.

Driving his body into hers after so many years of celibacy, he was unable to find the control he sought. But with Maggie control no longer seemed like something he needed.

He turned on his side and brought Maggie to hers. He drew her leg up over his hip.

"You humble me," he said, and stroked the inside of her thigh until she quivered. "I want to make you feel as incredible as you've made me feel."

She pressed her lips together with a moan, unable to speak as Jack stroked her, delved inside the folds, and moved upward to the most erotic spot of her body. The tiny pearl responded to the light strokes of his fingers, and Maggie pressed her face against his neck with a gasp of indrawn breath.

"Don't hide," he said. "I want to hear you." He stroked his tongue deep inside her mouth and mimicked the motions with his hand. Long fingers explored deeply in her body, while his thumb stroked elsewhere and took her to the edge.

Fingernails digging into his arms, Maggie cried out and clung to Jack. Her body pulsed around him, and his body roused again from her response. Turning her onto her back, he entered her while tremors still moved through her.

"Maggie," he whispered, as his body throbbed. Moments later he rocked into Maggie while she moved her hips with his. He crashed again, losing himself in Maggie.

Finally, the effects of the exhausting day overcame them. They curved together and slept while a soft rain danced on the roof.

CHAPTER TEN

MAGGIE shivered and pulled the blanket over her. Or tried to. But there was no blanket, and Jack slept curved into her back so she couldn't move without disturbing him. One hand pillowed her head and the other rested possessively on her hip, fingers splayed loose in sleep. His breathing fell slow and deep.

Before Maggie could stop it, a chill shot through her, and she shivered.

Jack stirred. "Cold?"

"A little."

Jack rose and got the other sleeping bag, unzipped it and draped it over them. "I want to hold you again," Jack said, climbing in beside her. "Is that OK?"

Maggie turned to face him and settled with her head on his shoulder. She closed her eyes. "Fine with me," she said, and sighed, more content than she'd ever been in her life. Her old memory was nowhere to be found.

Jack kissed the top of her head. "You feel wonderful against me," he whispered. "Thank you."

Hours later, morning came with a burst of rain in another storm on the heels of the first. Maggie woke to the smell of fresh coffee.

She popped her head out from beneath the cocoon of the sleeping bags. She sniffed and her mouth watered at the fragrance. "Is that really coffee I smell or am I hallucinating?" she asked, and watched as Jack moved around the small eating area. The smile on his face made her heart flip at the simple gesture.

"Are you ready for some?" he asked, and brought a cup to her.

Greedily she took the mug from him and sipped the scalding brew. "Thanks. I need my coffee in the mornings before I can move."

"Did you sleep well?" he asked, and watched her face, looking for something, he wasn't sure what.

"I slept great. Better than I have in years," she said, and he was satisfied with that. "Must be the fresh air out here," she said.

He laughed and it felt good. "You're such a tease," he said, and stroked her cheek with his hand. "I love that about you. You try to keep a sense of humor in a tense situation."

"Do you think this is tense?" she questioned, worried that the atmosphere between them was changing.

"No, tense was the wrong word. Unusual…unusual for both of us."

She sipped at the cup again. "Unusual is right. I've never been stranded in a fish camp in the wilds of Alaska before." She smiled. Then she sat upright, her eyes concerned. "My brother will be worried about me."

"I relayed a radio message to him and to Ella that we're OK." He squinted out the small window. "This secondary storm is going to keep us grounded for at least another day."

"Seriously?"

"Yes. Is that a problem for you?" He sipped his coffee and sat on the edge of the bed beside her.

"No. It's just strange. It's like we're in a totally different world out here. Alone. Weathered in. Are we co-workers or lovers now?" She looked up at him, her gaze questioning.

"Or both?" he said, and curved his fingers beneath her chin. "Can't we just enjoy this time for now?"

"Is it the same for you?"

"Kind of strange, surreal, wonderful and frightening all at the same time?"

She nodded.

He rose and turned away, uncomfortable with the direction of the conversation. "Are you game to try something new today?"

"Uh, sure. What did you have in mind?" She rose and put on her sweatshirt and pants.

"Did you see the fish wheel down on the river?"

"Fish wheel? I never heard of one, so I don't know if I saw it or not."

"It's basically a large scoop for fishing on the river. It turns like a wheel on a mill, but instead of scooping water, it scoops up fish."

"It's hard to envision, but I'll try it." She tied her boots and stood.

"Abel was concerned about not getting enough fish for his grandmother to dry for winter. I thought maybe we could do some fishing and take the catch up to their village."

"That's a wonderful idea," she said.

"Not afraid to get a little wet, are you?" The grin that burst onto his face was something he couldn't control.

She grinned and grabbed one of the slickers. "Not me. I'm from Boston, remember?"

They trekked through the rain upriver about a hundred yards to the fish wheel. Maggie looked at the flimsy contraption and then at Jack, her eyes wide. "Are you nuts? I'm not getting on that thing," she stated, and rooted her feet where they were.

Jack turned to face her and laughed, enjoying her reaction. "It's not as bad as it looks. Once you get on, it's pretty sturdy."

"Yeah, right. Selling bridges now, too, Jack?" She crossed her arms.

Jack moved to step out onto the framework dock and bobbled before he balanced on the wooden platform. "See?"

"If you think I'm getting on that…that…" She waved her hand in the direction of the wheel.

"We're doing this for those less fortunate than ourselves, remember?"

Maggie narrowed her eyes and glared at him. "That's just mean." She watched as he worked to set up the wheel and maneuver it into position. And her resistance dissolved. Jack was willing to do this for the Topsekok family. What was her problem? A little rain? A little physical labor? If she fell in the river, she'd just get wet. She was already wet. "OK. But if I fall in and get eaten by wild Alaska salmon, you're responsible, buddy," she said. Maggie picked her way through the tall grass at the edge of the river and waited for Jack to help her onto the platform.

Grinning the whole way to her side, Jack held out his hand and brought her onto the platform. "Thank you," he said, and then released her hand.

Maggie wobbled, losing her balance immediately, and Jack reached for her. With his hands on her waist to steady her, she grabbed the supports and held on. Looking up at Jack, his face so close to hers, she wanted to reach under the hood of the slicker and drag his mouth to hers. Instead, she clutched the wooden side. "I'm OK now."

Out in the middle of the river, they fished, using the primitive wheel, which was surprisingly effective, to scoop the fish. They settled into a rhythm, with Jack using his muscle to work the wheel and Maggie piling the fish to the side. They talked little during this time, but worked as a team. After several hours out in the river, Jack moved the platform to the shore and secured it in place.

By the end of the day Maggie had a new respect for lox and bagels. They loaded the fish into heavy-duty trash bags and packed ice from the coolers around them to keep until morning.

"The rain has finally quit," Jack said as he observed the sky beginning to lighten from black to grey.

"I love the rain, but I'm happy to see the sun again, too," Maggie said, and rinsed her hands in the river. "Ugh. I'm sure I'll smell like fish for a week," she said, and wrinkled her nose at the odor that lingered on her hands.

"Try some of this. It'll get the smell off your hands," Jack said, and tossed her a white tube.

"Toothpaste? Will it make my hands minty fresh, too?"

"Smart ass," Jack said with a grin. "Just do it."

After a few minutes of scrubbing with a glob of the green gel, Maggie was amazed at how easily it removed the fish smell. "Now, what about the rest of me?" she said, looking down at her mud-spattered clothing.

A squeal of surprise erupted from her as Jack scooped her up into his arms. He carried her to the edge of the dock and dangled her over the river.

"I have the solution for that." A mischievous grin lit his face, and Maggie clutched his shoulders.

"Jack Montgomery! If you drop me, I'll report you to the medical board."

"For what?" He scoffed at her threat and dipped her once.

"Nurse abuse."

"Abuse? You really think this is abuse?" he asked, his voice husky. His eyes turned dark, and Maggie recognized the burst of desire that shone in their dark depths as it quivered through her.

"You didn't think it was abuse last night," he said.

"Last night was different." She watched his mouth as he spoke. She imagined those lips feasting again on her body.

Jack released her legs, and she stood on the dock beside him, swaying with the movement of the river. His free arm drifted down to rest on her hip. A frown crept over his face, and he took a step back from her, his playful mood suddenly gone. Shoving his hands into his jacket pockets, he turned to face the river.

"What's wrong?" she asked, but refrained from touching him, as she longed to do.

"Nothing." He sighed. "I was going to build a fire

and cook one of the salmon for dinner. I can heat some water for you to bathe if you like."

"That would be wonderful," she said, wondering at the abrupt change that had overtaken him. She hoped it wouldn't last. The lighter side of Dr. Jack Montgomery was very appealing but, oh, so fleeting.

"It'll take a while, so I'd better get started."

Maggie watched him walk away toward the camp and let him go. The storm had kept the mosquitoes away, but now, with the rain and wind settled, they descended on her, intent on getting at every inch of exposed skin they could find. After swatting without effect at them, she ran to the camp and darted through the door.

To find Jack undressed, down to his underwear. Maggie stopped and gaped at him. "What are you doing?"

"Washing?" he said, and lifted the cloth in his hand. The self-deprecating look in his eyes tweaked her heart. "I figured the colder the water, the better."

Tearing her gaze away would have been difficult, so she didn't. She took the cloth from his hand and dipped it in the frigid bathing water. Soap applied, she moved to his back. Jack shivered and tried to pull away from the chill water. "Woman, are you trying to freeze me?" he said, as waves of goose-flesh crossed his body.

Maggie smiled. "You're the one who wanted a cold bath." She scrubbed his back and returned the cloth to the water. She prepared it again and applied it to his chest, washing his pecs, abdominals and up to his arms, watching the goose-bumps skate across his skin.

"You don't know what kind of torture this is," he said, and closed his eyes.

"Yes, I do."

When Jack opened his eyes, playtime was over. He grabbed her arms and pulled her to him.

Cold and wet and half-naked, he'd never wanted a woman more than he had at that moment. Last night they'd come together with a passion born of fear. Tonight frustrated anger consumed him. Anger pushed him to the edge of reason, and he took Maggie's mouth with his, pouring all the sexual frustration of the last two years into the kiss. Jerking away from her, he leaned on the table and almost tipped it over. "God, Maggie. Do you have any idea how much I want to make love to you again right now?"

"No."

He looked at her, taking in the way she held his gaze, the firm line of her jaw and the swollen lips. She tried to control her breathing, but he knew those deep breaths weren't because she'd just run a marathon. "Oh, I think you do."

"Why don't you tell me?"

"I'm standing here almost naked, dousing myself in ice water to freeze my desire for you. It's not just my body that wants you, Maggie. It's my heart, my mind. But I can't. Every time I look at you, something pulls at me, and not just physically. Making love with you last night was beautiful, and I needed it more than you'll ever know. But for both our sakes it has to be the only time."

"Why? Why does it have to end?" she asked, and started toward him. "Can't you give us a chance?"

"Long before I met you, I made a commitment."

"You need to *be* committed if you think you're the only man who's lost a wife, a mate, a lover—"

"I lost my life," he snapped, and his voice cracked.

"You didn't. You have a life. You're just afraid to live it."

Slack-jawed, Jack stared at her.

"You're afraid that reaching out to someone could get you hurt again, and it probably will. Well, welcome to the real world, pal. It ain't easy, but it's the only one we've got."

She stormed out of the cabin and left him standing there, dripping wet and alone, his mind more confused than he would ever have anticipated.

He'd been confused before about women in the past, so the current situation didn't really surprise him. When he'd first discovered what a woman really was, that had scared him, intrigued him and eventually baffled him. But he'd been young with an unbreakable heart. Or so he'd thought. Until Arlene. Their relationship had been easy. Maybe too easy. And when she'd died, he'd died, too. At least, that's what he'd wanted to do, prayed for it every night for months. But too many people had needed him and his skills as a doctor for him to give in to the luxury of overwhelming grief. So he'd buried himself in his work until the weeks and months had passed. By the time the initial numbness had worn off, he'd been so deeply embedded in work that he hadn't been able to grieve.

Jack dried himself and changed into fresh clothing. Digging into the supplies, he pulled out a hunk of cheese and a bottle of wine. Tucking the bottle under his arm, he left the cabin. Maggie stood on the dock again, against the backdrop of the newly blue sky, skirted on the horizon by departing stormclouds.

Thankfully, the light breeze kept the mosquitoes away. Unable to think of anything to say, he stopped behind her.

"I've been watching the most amazing wildlife show, Jack."

The soft amazement in her voice tugged at his heart.

With her arm outstretched, she pointed across the river. "A mama bear with two cubs is fishing over there." Her finger moved to another area. "Loons have been swimming in that area, although I can't see them very well. Their voices really pull at my heart, they're so melancholy." Then she pointed to an area far down the river. "And I think a moose is out there, eating river grass."

"Alaska is an amazing place." That she felt about his home the same way he did just about dropped him to his knees.

She turned and noticed what he carried. "Offering tokens of your questionable affection?" she asked, with a gentle look in her eyes and a sad smile on her face.

"It's all I have."

"It's all you'll offer."

"Can we take this slice of time and enjoy it for what it is?"

"What is it, Jack?" She took a glass from his hand and tipped it, waiting for him to pour wine into it. "A chance to be lovers with no strings attached? Nobody except us knows it happened, so it can't be real, right?"

They sat on the dock and drank the wine. Jack pulled out a pocket knife and sliced cheese for her. He fed it to her and watched as she chewed, then sipped the wine with the cheese still in her mouth. On impulse, he leaned into her, took her lips with his and tasted the intoxicating flavors mingled in her mouth. The kiss was gentle, sweet and powerful.

Jack filled her glass again and drank from his, keeping his gaze on her, wishing things could be different between them. "This slice away from reality is all I can give you. It's up to you whether you'll take it. Can you be my lover for another day, then return to Kodiak, forget this happened, and go on with your life?"

"Go on with my life? You mean, as in dating other men, maybe sleeping with them?" She chewed her cheese and contemplated him with the fire of challenge in her eyes.

The thought of another man touching Maggie and enjoying the pleasures of her body the way he had last night filled him with rage, but he had no right to it. "There are no strings attached to this time." Though it killed him, he had to say it. A bite of cheese, a sip of wine, a pinch of guilt.

Maggie stood. "I'm going to go wash up. I'll see you in a bit."

She left him sitting there with the glass paused halfway to his mouth. The incessant, infuriating buzz of the mosquitoes reflected his mood.

He tried to be patient while he finished the glass of wine and wrapped up the cheese. Some impulsive part of his nature wanted to guzzle the rest of the bottle down so that he had an excuse to forget about his commitment. But if losing his wife to cancer hadn't made him a drunk, the prospect of spending another night with Maggie shouldn't make him one either.

About thirty minutes passed before Jack returned to

the cabin. As he pushed the door open, a sheen of sweat appeared on his palms and he wiped it away. How could something like this make him nervous? How could something like this *not* make him nervous?

He entered the dimly lit cabin to find Maggie watching him from the table. She had brushed and re-braided her hair, washed and changed clothing.

A checker set lay open in front of her. Challenge glittered in her eyes.

"What are you doing?" he asked, and set the glasses and wine down.

"Waiting for you."

"For?" He let the question hang.

"Strip checkers."

Jack laughed and almost choked. "Are you serious?"

"Yep. I won the strip checker championship my freshman year of college, I'll have you know. To this day that record stands."

Doubtful, but intrigued, Jack stepped closer. "Strip checkers championship? How many layers of clothing did you wear?"

"That's my secret."

He moved closer still. "And how many layers do you have on now?" he asked, watching as she dropped her gaze from his and fiddled with the edge of the checkerboard. Moving behind her, he bent down to kiss the side of her neck and watched as the tiny hairs stood to attention. She wasn't unaffected by him. "Maggie?"

"Yes?"

"Do you really want to play checkers?" he asked, and licked her neck, intent on driving her mad.

"Wh-what?" A shiver made her shoulders quake.

"Strip checkers? Remember that?"

"Oh, yes," she said. "It was the only thing I could find to entertain ourselves with."

"Really? No books?" He moved to the other side, still behind her, and nuzzled that side of her neck.

"Why don't you come out from there?" she asked.

He sat opposite her.

"Your move," she said, throwing down the gauntlet.

CHAPTER ELEVEN

SEVERAL games of checkers later Jack shivered in his Jockeys and glared at Maggie. "You weren't kidding, were you?"

"About what?" she asked, and raised a brow, mock innocently batting her eyelashes at him.

"About being a champion checkers player."

"No. But the strip part was slightly embellished," she admitted. "I used to beat the pants, no pun intended, off my brother. Made him mad, too. That was the part I liked best." She grinned and stacked the checkers for a new game.

"He was very concerned about your safety."

"What do you mean?"

"He and Ella came to see me before I left. I had to delay flying out for a while, and I sat in the pub with them." Jack reached for his shirt and put it on. "He's really a nice guy and loves you a lot."

"He's OK as brothers go. I think I'll keep him."

"My brother and I used to beat the hell out of each other."

"You have just one brother?"

"And a sister." He made a move on the checkerboard, but his heart was no longer in it.

"Where are they?"

"Seattle area. They get up here once in a while or I go down there." He shrugged. "They've asked me to move closer to them since Arlene died, but it seemed like too much trouble at the time."

"Would you like to move someday?" She countered his move and took a checker.

"Under the right circumstances I suppose I would, but I haven't given it much thought."

They finished the game, both subdued. At the end, when Maggie took his last checker, she looked at him. "You let me win that one."

"My heart isn't in it, I guess." Suddenly restless, he moved away from the table and pulled on the rest of his clothing.

"I can't, Jack," Maggie whispered, clutching her hands together in her lap.

"Can't what?" he asked and turned.

"Can't be your lover and walk away like nothing happened. Last night meant something to me, but if all you want is sex, then you're looking for it in the wrong person."

A flash of anger shot through him, and he moved closer to her, placed his hands on her shoulders. "Last night meant something to me, too. More than you'll ever know. You made me feel like a man again, Maggie. Something I haven't felt since Arlene died. I'll always be grateful to you for that."

"Grateful?" She shoved away from him, her eyes bright with anger or unshed tears. "I don't want thanks. That's not why I slept with you."

"Why did you?"

"Because I wanted to." She huffed out a breath and tried not to give in to the tears behind her eyes.

"That's it?" It wasn't quite the response he'd anticipated.

"Isn't wanting to make love with you enough?" she asked. "I care about you, and I wanted you. I was frightened about being here alone, but that wouldn't make me jump into just anyone's bed. Being with you made me feel precious, Jack. That's hard to let go of. The last time I let a man close to me he humiliated me and I swore off men. Until you." Her lopsided smile tugged at him. "You made me feel special, Jack."

"You are special, Maggie." He stepped closer still and tucked a strand of hair behind her ear. This time he didn't hesitate. Performing the gesture somehow felt right now, he'd done it so many times. "You're a very special woman. You're caring and compassionate, an excellent nurse. You're funny and beautiful, and I've come to admire you in the short time you've been here."

"But?"

"But nothing. It's all true."

"You just can't think about having a real relationship with me."

There it was and he hated to disappoint her. "No. I can't have a real relationship with *anyone*, not just you."

"Then you're an idiot, Jack." Anger sparked in her eyes, masking her pain. "Do you know what you're giving up?"

"A chance for more heartache if something happens to you, or our relationship doesn't work out." He shook his head. "No, thank you. I've had enough heartache to last me a lifetime."

"Coward."

Jack spun to face her. "After what I went through to come for you in the middle of that storm, you can stand there and call me a coward? I wasn't sure I was going to make it here, Maggie. The storm could have overpowered my plane, I could have been struck by lightning, or gotten lost, and you're calling me a coward?" He grabbed her by the shoulders, but she pushed away from him.

"That was the easy part, wasn't it? Risking your life was nothing. Risking your heart is too much for you. I'll bet making love with me, though physically enjoyable, was tougher for you than to fly into that storm."

Speechless, he stared at her. "You have some nerve when all you've done is run from Daddy all of your life," he said, lashing out at her.

"Thanks to you I've stopped running, and I'm facing my demons. Why don't you take your own medicine, Doctor?" She turned away from him, and he let her go. "I'm going to bed. Goodnight."

The glance she threw at him was cold. He deserved it because she was right, dammit. He sat on the bed and removed his boots, then lay on top of the sleeping bag, contemplating Maggie's words. She rustled around, getting comfortable on the other bed. He listened to her breathing, but it never became even or deep.

"Are you awake?" he whispered.

"Yes."

"I'm sorry. I didn't mean to hurt you."

"I know."

But as he listened to her muffled breathing, he could tell she was crying. He sat up and went to her. Drawing her resistant body up, he pulled her onto his lap and rocked her.

Jack kissed the top of her head and pressed his cheek to hers as she held on to him, loving the feel of her body against his. "I wish I could make your hurt go away."

"You're the one who's hurt me, but you're the only one who can make it go away." She sniffed and wiped her face with the heels of her hands.

"Isn't that how relationships work, no matter what kind?"

"I guess." She slid from his lap and faced the wall. "Sorry."

"Don't be." The comfort he offered was a legitimate excuse to hold her in his arms again. Probably for the last time. "Let's get some sleep. We're going to have a busy day tomorrow." He moved to the other bed.

"Goodnight, Jack."

He lay on top of the sleeping bag, contemplating a spider crawling from its corner to investigate the camp. That lasted for about half an hour before Jack got up and went outside. Maybe the sugar in the wine kept him from sleeping. Maybe sleeping in an unfamiliar place made him restless. Or maybe anticipation about returning to Kodiak tomorrow wouldn't let his brain turn off. In the past none of those things had ever affected his sleep. He glanced back at the cabin, remembering the way Maggie slept. What he wouldn't give to crawl into that sleeping bag with her and discover all the nuances of her body he'd missed last night.

He'd give anything, but would he give *up* anything

for her? Could he give up Arlene? Curling his hands into fists, he stared out at the river, calm again now that the storm had passed. Tied to the dock, the plane bobbed gently. They'd take off in it tomorrow and return to reality. That thought saddened him more than it ever had before. After being away, he'd always looked forward to going home, but not after this trip. This trip was different.

If he had his way, he'd stay at this primitive camp in the wilderness locked away with Maggie for ever. Out here he could forget and just live like the man he wanted to be. Back in Kodiak too many reminders of his past life with Arlene prevented him from moving on.

Maybe he should leave the island and start a new life somewhere else, as his family had often suggested. But he wasn't sufficiently motivated to uproot his life and start over. Starting over was for a generation younger than his.

A noise behind him made him turn quickly. Danger was never far away in Alaska. And there it was, staring him down.

Maggie stood on the dock behind him, wrapped in a spare blanket. She was the most dangerous and most beautiful woman he'd ever come across.

"Are you all right?" She blinked, her eyes soft and sleepy.

"Yes. Just getting some air."

"Oh. I thought maybe you couldn't sleep, like me."

"Having trouble?" he asked, and put an arm around her shoulders, unable to resist drawing her against his side.

"Yes. Returning to Kodiak is bothering me."

"Why?"

"I've enjoyed our time away, and I can't say I'm eager to go back." She shrugged. "Jamie's there. He'll ask questions about us. He's very perceptive."

"You don't have to defend yourself to anyone, not even your brother," he said, the idea irritating him.

She looked up at him, her big blue eyes captivating him. "Let's go back in. I'm cold."

Once inside she wrapped herself up in a blanket and crawled inside the sleeping bag. She huddled there, trying to stay warm and trying not to give in to the urge to call out to Jack, trying not to trade her convictions for physical need.

She knew he could satisfy her. He'd proved that last night. But the needs of her physical body didn't compare to the needs of her soul, her heart and her spirit. He'd proved that he wouldn't satisfy those needs.

Trying not to cry, she faced the wall and attempted to sleep.

When morning came, the smell of coffee hung heavy in the air. Jack was already up and had some of their gear packed in the plane.

"C'mon, Maggie. We're burning daylight, and we've got a lot to do." Jack jiggled her awake.

"What time is it?" she asked.

"Doesn't matter. The sun's up."

"The sun's up at midnight, too," she complained.

He passed a cup of coffee near her nose, rousing her from her sleepy state.

She sat up, reaching for the cup.

"We've got to get to Chinook Falls and deliver the fish. Then we return to Kodiak."

Memories of the last two days flooded her. She drew on the stout brew to give her strength to get through this one.

After a hurried breakfast and another cup of coffee, Maggie dressed and stowed her belongings in the plane. And then they were off.

Sunlight glinted off the surface of the water as they followed the river north to the tiny village of Chinook Falls. The trip took about half an hour by plane, but it would have taken the Topsekoks many hours to reach their camp by vehicle.

Jack landed the plane on a clear stretch of the river and taxied to the docks. An elderly man helped tie it up.

"Thanks for the help," Jack said, and shook hands with the man, then assisted Maggie from the plane.

"Any time. That's some plane you got there," the old-timer said, admiring the single-prop plane.

"It's a special medical transport plane. We're looking for the family of Elmer Topsekok—do you know them?"

"Sure. Out here everyone knows everyone or is related to them," he said. "You and the missus come with me, and I'll take you to Mrs. Topsekok. She don't speak no English, though." The man led the way through the village on bowed legs that had probably suffered a case of rickets. In this wilderness fresh fruit or a source of vitamin D were hard to come by, and many people suffered from nutritional diseases.

The man led Jack and Maggie to a frame house, knocked on the door and introduced the couple to Mrs. Topsekok in her own language.

"We have a load of fish for her. Her husband has been

injured, and he's been shipped to Anchorage for surgery. He'll be fine, but needs to spend some time there recovering. We brought the fish for her family because he couldn't bring it himself."

The man translated. Maggie could see a range of expressions and emotions flow over the woman's face. Shock and disbelief were followed by relief. She grabbed Jack, pulled him into a fierce hug, and did the same to Maggie. Rushing into the house, she returned with a sea-grass basket about the size of a small tissue box. It had a small lid on it and a blue and green design woven into it.

"She made this and wants to give it to you as a small gesture of thanks," the guide said.

Maggie took it in her hands, afraid she was going to crush the delicate basket. The skill needed to produce a product of this detail took decades to master.

"That's some gift. Some of her baskets are in the Smithsonian," the man said.

"Please, thank her for me. I will treasure this," Maggie said, and clutched the basket to her chest. Maggie leaned down to kiss the gnarled cheek of the woman and was rewarded with a pat on her face by a work-roughened hand.

After the fish were unloaded and the plane refueled, a boy of about ten years old with eyes as black as obsidian and hair to match raced to them. He tugged at Jack's sleeve. "Are you the doctor man?" he asked.

Jack bent down to match the boy's height. "Yes, I'm the doctor man. Do you need a doctor?"

"No, my grandpa does," the boy said, and started off down the street.

"Wait," Jack called. "I need my medicine bag." The boy waited impatiently as Jack retrieved a medical supply bag from the plane. He and Maggie trekked along as they were led to a house. From outside they could hear someone coughing inside. Maggie and Jack exchanged a concerned look and then entered the home.

"In here." The boy pointed to a small bedroom. "He's sick bad."

Jack knelt on the floor beside a man debilitated by emphysema, his barrel chest having changed over the years to accommodate the disease process. The man coughed deeply again and spat up blood.

"He might have TB," Maggie said, and grabbed face masks for them to put on.

"I know. Unfortunately, it's making a big comeback up here," Jack said, and reached for his stethoscope to listen to the man's lungs. Jack shook his head and didn't need to listen for long. "On top of that, he's got pneumonia."

"Is that bad?" the kid asked, his eyes wide as he watched Jack.

"What's your name?" Jack asked the boy.

"Amos George."

"Well, Amos, your grandpa is sick bad and should go to the hospital. We can have him flown to Anchorage and they'll take good care of him."

"Is there anyone else to help you?" Maggie asked, wondering if the boy was alone with his grandpa.

"My mom. But she works in the market sometimes."

"The store in the village?" Maggie asked.

"Tell her I'll call Anchorage and send a plane for him. We can't help him in Kodiak for what he's got," Jack said.

"OK," Amos said, looking frightened, his breath puffing through trembling lips. "Thank you."

As they left the house another woman approached them about an ill family member. Jack and Maggie made recommendations and left.

"This is astounding," Maggie said, her pace slowing as they neared the plane.

"What is?" Jack watched her.

"So many sick people and the total lack of medical care in the village. It's appalling." Maggie had never encountered such poor people who lived on the edge of society and on the edge of the wilderness. They couldn't just go to the next town for care. The next town was hundreds of miles away over impassable mountains.

"It's not something that people who live in remote areas have ever had or expect to have."

"But couldn't the state or the government do something about it?" The idea of having absolutely no medical care had never occurred to Maggie until now.

"Like what?"

"Like build a clinic for these people."

"And who do you propose will run it?"

"Surely someone would live here, wouldn't they?"

"Would you?" he asked.

Maggie looked around the village before answering. There were no trees. The landscape was barren and very different from Kodiak Island. The village consisted of two churches, a post office and a small market, with houses interspersed between them. There wasn't even a bar. A community center was the largest building in town. "I don't think I personally would, but what about...?" Maggie's voice trailed off.

"It's a whole different lifestyle up here, isn't it?" Jack watched her as she took it all in.

"Yes, it is."

"I can't even find an anesthesiologist full time for the Kodiak clinic. There's no way a doctor would live out here full time."

"But what about a locum, a PA or a nurse practitioner? There must be someone who could do it?"

Jack paused, considering her suggestion. "That we might be able to get, but there's no clinic for a locum to work out of at this point."

"Maybe we can work on getting them one." With that idea in mind, Maggie's attitude changed and determination stiffened her spine. "Let's go to the community center and see if there's anyone else who needs help right now."

Jack followed her, admiring her courage and willingness to help these people. But when winter set in, he knew she would not want to stay there. Her determination wouldn't last through the harsh months.

Jack and Maggie set out on the return trip to Kodiak after seeing a total of eighteen patients. They all needed medical care unavailable in the village.

Maggie concentrated on taking in the beauty of the scenery below to distract herself. Tundra rolled in gentle slopes, covered with bushes and grasses, but little in the way of real trees. The landscape seemed barren at first glance, but as she watched, the life within the barrenness peeked out here and there, determined to survive, no matter what the circumstances.

"Are you OK?" he asked.

"Fine. I was just wondering if I dreamed the last few days. It's difficult to think about going back to civilization again, isn't it? I hate leaving those people without proper care," she said, and clutched the sea-grass basket to her. She would treasure it always.

"Yes. But you weren't dreaming." He clasped her hand and held it a moment, needing that tempting connection with her again before returning both hands to the controls.

Facing the front again, Maggie closed her eyes and tried to prepare herself for their landing in the real world. But she couldn't get the images of the villagers out of her mind, how poor they were, how little they had. But they were happy. At least, they looked happy. With the money she was turning down from her inheritance, these people could really benefit. An idea came to her, but before she could thoroughly explore it, Jack interrupted her thoughts.

"We're going to be landing in a few minutes," he said.

Maggie blew out a nervous breath and watched Jack. "Here comes reality, ready or not."

CHAPTER TWELVE

WITHIN an hour of landing in Kodiak, they had become celebrities. At least, on a small scale. Many of the villagers and hospital staff arrived to welcome them back from their unexpected adventure. They were unceremoniously dragged to the pub for celebratory toasts to Maggie's courage when she'd stayed behind for the sake of a patient. Jack's bravery for flying into the storm to rescue Maggie was toasted, as was his equal stupidity for flying into the storm to rescue Maggie.

A newspaper reporter took photos of the couple and interviewed them for an article. Maggie was more interested in notifying the public of the poverty in Chinook Falls than in discussing her rescue. Hours later she dragged herself home, dropped her clothing at the door of the bathroom and drowned herself in the shower for half an hour. When she emerged in her bathrobe from the billows of steam, Ella was home.

The woman grabbed Maggie and pulled her into a fierce hug. "Girl, I'm so glad you're home safe," Ella said. "You two scared the wits out of me and half the town." There were actually tears in her eyes, though she quickly turned away from Maggie.

"I'm glad to be back, too. It was a wild couple of days. Seems like a week passed."

"You aren't kidding," Ella said. "Your brother and I sat in the pub, drinking all the way through the first storm. By the second one we had to go get something to eat, so we stayed at the diner most of the day."

Maggie gaped. "You and Jamie drank together?"

Ella nodded and led Maggie to the couch. "Sure did. That boy can hold his liquor, too."

"I'm amazed," Maggie said, shaking her head.

"That he can drink?"

"No. That he would drink in the pub. He's more a country club kind of guy."

"Well, he held his own at the pub. You'd think he'd been going there all his life. Didn't embarrass himself once."

"Wow." Maggie removed the towel from her head and finger-combed the long wet strands out while she chatted with Ella.

"So, how was your time with Jack?" Ella asked.

"It was OK, I guess." She moved and her long hair covered her face.

"You guess?"

Maggie sighed and pushed the hair back. "He's still deeply committed to Arlene and isn't letting go any time soon, if that's what you meant."

"It was." Ella sighed. "I was kind of hoping you two would come to an understanding while you were away."

"An understanding?" Maggie's mouth went dry and her heart paused.

"You know." Ella gave Maggie a saucy look and twitched her brows.

"Ella McGee," Maggie said in a haughty tone, but couldn't meet Ella's eyes. Feeling as if she'd just bitten into a fiery red pepper, Maggie's face flamed at Ella's innuendo. Unable to answer the woman without an outright lie, Maggie stood. "Don't get your hopes too high on that one," she said. "Excuse me, Ella, but I've got to dry my hair, and then I'm going to bed. I'm exhausted."

"Didn't get much sleep while you were gone?" Ella asked.

"No," Maggie admitted.

"Aha! Something did happen, didn't it?" Ella's eyes narrowed to slits as she studied Maggie.

"Wh-what do you mean?" Maggie stared wide-eyed and tried not to betray anything.

"If you didn't get much sleep, what were you doing when you were supposed to be sleeping?"

"We went fishing."

"Fishing? That's a new one." She snorted.

"No, really. We used the fish wheel on the river at the camp and flew a whole planeload of salmon to the patient's family up river. That whole village is so poor, it's appalling. No wonder they were worried about getting that fish home."

"Which village?" Ella asked.

"Chinook Falls."

Ella shook her head and clucked her tongue. "I know the place, and you're right. I wish we could help them out."

"Jack and I saw a bunch of patients while we were there, but they could all use additional medical care."

"Maybe we can do something for them here in

Kodiak. Have a fundraiser of some kind and send the proceeds to them."

"Do you think they would take an outright gift like that?" Maggie said. "Most people are too proud."

"Those people are just trying to survive." Ella paused a minute. "There used to be a cannery there that employed hundreds of people, but it closed down twenty years ago and the village almost died. Those folks are all that's left."

"That's so sad. I hope we can help them."

"Me, too."

Maggie yawned and stretched. "I've really got to get some sleep." She patted Ella's shoulder. "Thanks," she murmured as she drifted down the hall and shut her door.

Ella stared after her, wondering if all Maggie had said was true. She wanted her and Jack to get together. Maybe they just needed a little more help.

The next day was Jamie's last night in town, so he and Maggie shared a farewell dinner.

"You know what I'm going to do, don't you?" Jamie asked at the end of the meal.

"What do you mean? Do about what?"

"I'm going to spend the rest of our evening together trying to lure you back home into the fold of wealth, power and influence."

"You know those things mean little to me."

"I know, but Father doesn't. He's going to be all over me for not bringing you back, so I've got to at least be able to say I tried."

Maggie grinned, pleased he wasn't going to take

their father's side and make her choose between her family and her job, her new life. "I appreciate that."

"After seeing you here in this environment, I think you're right. You do fit in well." He sipped his wine. "But doesn't school appeal to you any longer?"

"No. I have my bachelor's degree and that's enough for me. At least for now." She looked down at her plate and toyed with the fork.

"If there's something you're interested in, why wait? You should apply to school right away. The longer you wait, the harder it will be to go back."

"I know. But I'm enjoying being away from a university setting for a change. This is hard to let go of for all the wonder of school again," Maggie said, sarcasm dripping from her words.

"Father would pay for you to return to school if you came home."

"I know. But this is something I want to do on my own." She leaned forward, hoping to pour some of her intensity into him. "I need to do this, for me."

"What is it?"

"CRNA school."

"What the heck is that?" he asked.

"Certified Registered Nurse Anesthetist school."

"Meaning?" Jamie's eyes registered only confusion.

"Meaning I could administer anesthesia for operations, conscious sedation for small procedures, and pain control for people with chronic pain. In a place like this, anesthesiologists are hard to find and keep. Having a skill like anesthesia would make me really marketable, and I could go anywhere, if I wanted to."

"But you want to stay in Alaska."

"Yes, though I couldn't go to school here. The closest school is in Seattle, so I'd have to go there."

Jamie looked around. The expression on his face reminded her of their father, and she waited for him to speak. "This place is so small…"

"You haven't seen small until you've been to the village Jack and I went to. They have nothing up there. Not even a fast-food restaurant."

Jeremy looked shocked.

"God, I know I couldn't live there." He shuddered. "No quality coffee around any given corner to satisfy my every whim? You're welcome to it." He flagged down the waiter. "A *latté* please. Do you want one, Maggie?"

"No. Plain coffee is fine. So, what are you going to tell Father when you get back?" Right now she didn't care. She'd grown in the last weeks and now she knew she was stronger than she'd ever been in her life. Even standing up to her father seemed like a challenge she could handle.

"I've already been emailing him, telling him about your adventures."

Maggie sat up straight. "What have you told him?"

Jamie smiled. "That you seem to have found your place in the world." He sat back and raised one eyebrow. "Possibly even found a love interest."

"Love interest?" The muscles in her throat contracted, and she almost choked.

"Yes. Of course, I had to tell him all about Dr. Montgomery so he could do a background check and make sure the man's not just after your money."

"Jamie! Jack couldn't care less about my money."

Maggie covered her face with her hands and groaned. "Please, tell me you didn't do that." The silence continued until Maggie looked up.

Jamie grinned. "Think I'd do that to you, little sister?"

She clutched his hand and squeezed. "You scared the life out of me. Had that been true, I would have been mortified if Jack had found out."

"Anyway, no worries from me. Of course, Father's going to be disappointed that you're not returning and may try to coerce you into coming home, but I'll try to intervene."

"You will?" Tears pricked Maggie's eyes. She and Jamie had been close growing up, but having him support her against their father's influence made her appreciate that relationship even more. "Thank you," she whispered. "It means a lot to me to stay here."

"I know. I can't promise he won't be on the phone to give you a royal piece of his mind, but you've got my support."

"You're a great brother."

"Now that I'm agreeing with you, you say that. Do you remember how many times we argued as kids, and you hated my very existence?"

"I'm your little sister. I was *supposed* to hate your very existence."

Jamie leaned back in his chair as their coffees arrived.

"Father's money doesn't appeal to me, but there is something he could do with it *for* me."

"What's that?"

"The village Jack and I visited needs a free clinic."

Jamie scoffed, nearly spewing his *latté*. "You know Father won't put money into something that he doesn't get a return on."

Maggie leaned forward, now fierce in her passion about the subject. "But he could name it after himself. And charitable donations are tax deductible. He knows that." She contemplated Jamie, wondering if he would go for the idea that had been forming in her mind since the trip to Chinook Falls. "And it would go a long way to show me he's willing to compromise with me."

"Compromise? Our father?" Jamie felt for her pulse. "Are you feeling all right?"

"Be serious," she said, and playfully slapped his hand.

"I am. And you are seriously delusional if you think he would go to that length to get into your good graces. He doesn't work that way. The world revolves around him, remember?"

"See what you can do. You make your living working business deals. See what you can do with this one." The waiter brought the check, and Jamie gave the man a credit card without looking at the bill.

They left the restaurant and stood outside in the midnight sun. "I don't know how you'll get used to this light thing," he said with a shake of his head.

"I want to, so I will."

"My flight is early in the morning, so I'll say goodbye tonight."

They embraced, and Maggie clung to him for just a moment, knowing it would be a long time until they saw each other again. "Thank you, Jamie. I appreciate you so much. And I love you, too."

Jamie pulled back and cleared his throat. "Yes. Well. I love you too, little sister." He kissed her cheek. "Take care of yourself, and try to stay out of trouble."

"I will. Be safe." Maggie turned and walked the few blocks home without incident, wondering if he would talk to their father on her behalf. In the meantime, she had a shift to work in the morning.

The next morning Maggie walked into chaos in the clinic. People ran back and forth to patient rooms. Call lights buzzed incessantly and the phone rang as soon as the secretary replaced it.

"What's going on?" she asked, and shoved her purse beneath the nurses' station.

"Gigantic case of food poisoning from a family reunion yesterday," one of the night shift nurses replied on her way to the utility room.

"Oh, man. That's so gross," Maggie said. But she jumped into the fray and carried spit buckets, bedpans and clean linen. None of the staff rested for hours. When Catherine passed by, Maggie took a bag of dirty linen from her. "This is too heavy for you! You need to go to the lounge and rest for a little while," Maggie said, and gave Catherine a friendly push in that direction.

"But—"

"I'll cover for you. It'll be fine. I'll come get you in fifteen minutes."

But that time came and went before Maggie realized that she'd forgotten Catherine and the woman hadn't returned. Maggie found Catherine curled up in a ball on the sofa in the lounge. "What's wrong?" She rushed to her friend's side.

"I'm losing the baby," she sobbed.

"Are you bleeding?"

"Just spots."

"Any cramping?" Maggie asked.

Catherine nodded. "A few. But this is how it always starts."

"If I remember correctly, it's not uncommon to have a little spotting in the first three months." She helped Catherine to sit up. "Now, go wash your face. You can sit and answer the phone or something." Maggie left the lounge and came face to face with Jack.

"Oh, hi, Jack."

"What's going on? Where are you and Catherine? We're busy as hell out there."

"I know. She'll be out in a minute. She needed a break, and I saw to it that she got one."

"*You* did? You're not the charge nurse today."

"No, I'm not. But that's not the point."

"What is the point?"

"I'm concerned that Catherine's not getting enough rest and is working too hard. Can we send her home for the rest of the day?"

"With the clinic full of sick patients? No way. We're trying to find more staff to come in." Jack frowned. "If Catherine's not pulling her weight, I'll have to have a chat with her."

"You will not," she said, and grabbed Jack by the sleeve. She led him to a remote area of the clinic, away from any eavesdroppers. "You will leave her alone. If something needs to be done, I'll do it for her."

"What's going on? Catherine's perfectly able to handle the work on her shift."

"She can't do any lifting, and she needs frequent rest periods." How much could she tell Jack without giving away Catherine's secret?

"What are you talking about? Is she ill?"

Maggie huffed out a sigh of resignation and closed her eyes for a second. She had to trust Jack with Catherine's secret. "She's pregnant, Jack. She's already had two miscarriages and is afraid she's losing this one. She's spotting."

Jack stepped back from Maggie. "Pregnant?"

"Yes."

"You're sure?"

"Yes. But she's spotting now and is quite upset. She needs to rest."

"Absolutely." He frowned. "Maybe I need to examine her."

"No. No one else but us knows she's pregnant, and until she gives us leave it's going to stay a secret."

He pulled a hand through his hair and sighed. "OK. But how are we going to cover her absence?"

"I can cover her patients until you can find another nurse to come in."

"Agreed."

But after another hour Jack hadn't found anyone else to come in. Everyone was out playing today. He gave Maggie the bad news. "I'm afraid we're going to be short-staffed for the rest of the shift."

"It's only eleven a.m."

"I know. It's going to be a long day. I'm sorry."

"What most of these people need is just IV fluids for hydration, Phenergan for the nausea, and let the bug run its course."

"That seems logical. Just what I would do. Good call."

"So unless something urgent comes in, that means you're relatively free, doesn't it?" Maggie asked, and looked Jack up and down his length with her sharp gaze.

"Sure, but—"

"Roll up your sleeves, Doctor. You're about to be demoted to nursing assistant."

"What? I can't possibly…" He stopped at the narrow-eyed look Maggie laid on him, and he swallowed.

"Are you too good to empty some spit buckets or haul laundry sacks?"

"No, but—"

"No buts. Get to work."

Maggie showed Jack a side of medicine he'd never really thought about. He'd always known someone did the dirty work. Now he was doing it. He emptied trash bins, changed linen bags when they overflowed and took the full ones to the laundry room. He even changed a few bedpans for those too infirm to get up and almost threw up himself, but he managed.

Maggie watched as he completed every task she assigned to him without complaint. And he did a thorough job of each chore. She approached Jack as warmth flowed in each pulse of her heart, though she tried to harden herself against softer emotions where he was concerned. "The shift's almost over, Jack, and everyone looks like they're going to make it. No signs of respiratory failure in any of them. Just the yucks. We can start discharging them to go home for the rest of their recovery."

"That sounds good." He wiped his forearm over his forehead and grinned.

"You did great today. I'm really proud of you," Maggie said. Against her better judgment she pulled him close for a quick hug.

"Careful. I'm a mess," he said, but his arms went around her.

"I don't care. Thank you," she said, and kissed his cheek. "Today would have been hell without you."

"You're welcome." Jack grinned at her pleasure in something so simple. But being part of a team meant doing things you weren't accustomed to when times were tough. He'd discovered that all over again today. Having Maggie lead him through the steps humbled him.

"Why don't you go wash up and get ready to sign discharge instruction sheets? I'll get them ready for those who are doing best." She started to walk away.

"Maggie?"

"Yes?"

"Thanks for asking me to help. It opened my eyes to a lot of things I've taken for granted."

"Really?" she asked with a sideways smile.

"Really."

"I'm glad I could help open your eyes about something, Jack." She just wished she could open his eyes to allowing himself to love again.

The stack of charts piled on the desk required completion before they could end the shift. But more than two hours later she was still at it, trying to get as many people out of the clinic and home as possible so that the night shift didn't have to take all the overflow.

"Why are you still here?" Jack asked, as he took a last walk through the clinic, amazed it was as clean and organized as it was after the hell that had occurred there today. That was thanks to Miss Maggie Wellington who had stepped up to the plate and hadn't run from trouble.

"There's too much to do yet for me to just go home."

"Isn't that why we have more than one shift, Maggie?" he asked. "Exhausting yourself won't do your patients any good."

"Yes, but—"

"But nothing. It's time for you to go home. Night shift can finish up. Besides, I know you haven't eaten anything since lunch and it's almost nine p.m."

"You're right. I could use something." Maggie patted her stomach, but as she made the gesture another thought occurred to her. "I wonder how Catherine's doing?"

"Why don't you call her?" Jack suggested, not liking the distress in Maggie's eyes.

"I could. But if she's asleep, I don't want to wake her up."

"That's considerate of you." He sat on the desk. "I know it's late, but do you want to get something to eat at the diner before you go home?"

"With you?" she asked.

"Yes."

"You buying?" Maggie grinned.

"Yes." Jack couldn't help but respond to that infectious grin.

"I'd love to."

They walked in silence to the diner, and Maggie tried to stifle a yawn. Jack noticed and grinned. "Tired, eh?"

"Yes. I haven't slept enough this week, and it's catching up with me."

They sat in a corner booth away from the stragglers.

"Ella was suspicious about us on the fish camp trip," Maggie whispered.

"Suspicious?"

"Maybe that's too strong of a word. She was more like hopeful."

"Really?"

"She wants us to get together."

"Maggie—"

She held up her hand to stop him. "I know. You don't have to tell me again. I told her there was no chance of that happening."

They finished the meal talking only about work, clinical issues and safe neutral topics. Maggie said nothing about wanting her father to open a clinic in Chinook Falls. Why bother? If her father didn't come through, no one would be disappointed except herself.

Jack's pager went off, and he answered the clinic's call on his cell phone. Thirty seconds into the call he hung up, tossed some money on the table and grabbed Maggie's arm.

"We've got to go. Catherine's losing the baby and she's hemorrhaging."

Maggie clutched Jack's hand as they raced back to the clinic. "Dammit, I knew I should have called her."

"Where is she?" Jack called, as they burst through the doors.

"Trauma three," Gloria said, and hurried after them.

Despite the long shift, Maggie ran to help her friend. She rushed to Catherine's side and clasped her friend's hand. "It's going to be OK, honey. Jack and I will take good care of you."

Catherine clutched Maggie's hand as if it were a lifeline. "I think I've already lost the baby. I passed some tissue, but I'm still bleeding heavily," she said, tears flooding her face.

"Jack's going to have to check you to see if you're still pregnant, and we'll run blood work, too."

"Don't worry right now about anything. Maggie and I are here with you," Jack said.

Maggie turned to him. She'd never heard him use such a soft, compassionate tone with anyone. An ache in her chest throbbed in response.

"Who's your doctor?" Jack asked.

"Sara McGuire. But she's on leave for two weeks."

"Is there someone on call for her?" Jack snapped on a pair of sterile gloves, and Maggie squirted lubricant into his hand.

"No. The other doctor she's with is on maternity leave and their practice is so small…" Catherine clutched her stomach. "Ouch."

Jack examined Catherine. "I'm sorry, but you were right. I can't feel the baby. You're still bleeding a lot and probably have some retained tissue that needs to come out. I'll set up your transport to Anchorage."

"No. Can't you do it here?" Distressed, Catherine came up onto her elbows.

"No. There's no one to run anesthesia, and I'm not a gynecologist. It's been years since I've done a D and C."

"Jack," Maggie interrupted. "I can keep her sedated.

Conscious sedation was something we did commonly at my last job, and I'm certified to administer it."

Jack frowned, and considered Maggie's statement. He started to shake his head. "I don't know if we can take the risk. What if something goes wrong?"

"It's not like you're going through her abdomen and need the higher-level anesthesia. But with a heart monitor, an IV and the right dosing of meds, I can keep her comfortable and out long enough for you to do the procedure."

"I can do it, but Catherine has to agree," Jack said.

"I agree. I agree. I'm in too much pain to make the flight for something you can do right here and now." She reached for Jack's hand. "Please, do this for me," she whispered. "I don't want to leave my home to have this done by strangers."

"Sign the consent, and I'll do it. Where's your husband?"

"Out on a fishing trip." Catherine's chin trembled and Maggie stroked Catherine's hair back from her face.

"It'll be OK. I promise," Maggie said, and offered what she hoped was a comforting smile. "Jack and I will take care of you."

"You're a good friend," Catherine whispered.

Minutes later everyone was ready.

"What's your plan?" Jack asked. Though he didn't outwardly betray it, Maggie knew he was nervous. The set of his jaw and the focus in his gaze told her.

"I start with small increments of Fentanyl for the pain and a few milligrams of Versed for amnesic effects, titrate to her response and keep her out." She turned to Catherine. "Do you have any allergies?" Maggie asked.

"No."

"Just listen to the sound of my voice and leave all your worries behind. Take a deep breath in and out," Maggie said, and injected the first micrograms of Fentanyl into the IV line. Maggie kept up a soothing verbal stream of nothing that Jack found as soothing as his patient. Catherine's eyes drooped, and Maggie kept her gaze on the heart monitor. After several minutes Catherine breathed slow and deep. "Night-time, Catherine." Maggie turned to Jack. "She's under."

"Good work," Jack said, his gaze lingering a moment on Maggie, wondering what he'd ever done without her.

CHAPTER THIRTEEN

AFTER the procedure Maggie eased up on the sedation and sat with Catherine, stroking her hair as the medication wore off. Near two a.m., Catherine stirred.

"Is it over?" she asked, and tried to focus on Maggie.

"All over, Sleeping Beauty," Maggie said, her heart aching for Catherine's loss.

"So much for that pregnancy."

"I know this is tough on you, but try to get some rest."

"I will." She squeezed Maggie's hand. "Thanks."

"You're welcome. I'll stay with you tonight, if you like," Maggie offered.

"Don't you work tomorrow?"

"Jack switched me with another nurse, so I'm off."

"I'll be OK. Go home and get some rest. Brittany is on tonight, and she'll look in on me."

"She's been in several times to check on you already. But I'll be back in the morning to see you."

"I'll be fine, and I can go home in the morning."

Jack pulled back the curtain and entered the cubicle. His hair stood on end in clumps, sleep wrinkles marred his face, and he shook his hand as if it had fallen asleep.

The man had never looked better to her. "How's our patient, Maggie?"

"Vitals are good, just a little bleeding, and she's roused nicely from the sedation without nausea or vomiting."

"You two make a great team," Catherine said.

Jack considered her words and looked at Maggie, his gaze never wavering. "You did a really good job with this."

"Thanks." A blush warmed her neck and crept into her face.

"She's great," Catherine said, without opening her eyes. "Give her a raise. A really big one."

Jack chuckled. "I'll think about it. We'll come back in the morning." Jack and Maggie left the room. "Want me to drive you home?"

"Yes. If you don't mind, I'd be grateful. It's been a long day."

In a few minutes they pulled up to Maggie's door. "I meant it when I said you did a great job back there," Jack said, his hands clutching the steering-wheel.

"I was shaking the whole time. I'm still shaking now." She held up a hand that visibly trembled.

"You never showed it. That's a sign of a real pro." He sighed and rubbed a hand over his face. "And I have to apologize to you."

Surprise lifted her brows. "For what?"

"For being an ass when we first met. I misjudged you based on your looks and your lack of field medicine." He took one of her hands in his. "But you have other fine skills that we need here."

"We?"

"Yes. The clinic." He cleared his throat and looked away, unable to speak aloud the feelings he had for her. Doing so would only get both of them hurt. "I'm releasing you from your probation."

"What do *you* need, Jack?"

"I've given up on my needs. They're irrelevant."

She faced him in the seat and turned a glare on him. "I disagree. If you're suffering from mental or emotional distress, I don't think you can be as good at your job as you could be. If you're happy, you'll be happier at your work, even if you hate it."

He grabbed her by the shoulders, all of the emotions he'd held back gnawing at his gut, clawing to get out. "You are the only one who has made me want to betray my vows. The only one."

"You're not betraying your vows by having a relationship with someone. Your wife is gone. You're not. Can't you see what's right in front of you, Jack?"

"What is right in front of me?" he asked, his words a husky whisper filled with electricity that sizzled over her.

"Me."

Jack buried his hands in her hair and kissed her. This was one of those long, slow, hot kisses, designed to rouse lustful desire. Jack's lips melted against hers and without any effort he eased her mouth open for his tongue to lure hers into a silken dance of desire. In no hurry, Jack dragged her across the seat and all the way onto his lap. Maggie lay across his chest and gave in to the magical sensations Jack Montgomery's mouth stirred. The glide of his lips across hers, the slow heat generated by his tongue made her want to make love to him with an ache, deep in her soul, that had never been satisfied by anyone except him.

He stroked her face, her neck and his hand roamed over her breasts as if memorizing their shape and how they fit in his hand. He lifted his head.

"Come home with me tonight," Jack whispered. "I want you to stay with me."

Maggie opened her eyes and stared at Jack's face, inches from her own. His eyes shone with desire for her. She was sure that her gaze reflected the same need, but that wasn't the only need she had for Jack. "I can't."

"You aren't working in the morning," he said. "No one will have to know you were at my place."

Maggie slid from his lap and returned to her seat with a sigh. "That's just it, Jack. It doesn't matter to me if anyone knows or not. Not that I'm going to shout from the rooftops, 'I slept with Jack Montgomery.' I'd know."

"Does anyone know?" he asked.

"No."

"Good. That's best."

"Best for who?" Maggie asked.

Jack raked his hair. "You want promises I can't give you, Maggie. You're asking too much of me."

"I don't want promises. There are no guarantees in life, and I wouldn't ask you for one. I'm only asking you for a chance. A chance to love you without restrictions." Maggie opened the door and stepped out. "I'm sorry." She closed the door of the Jeep and ran into the house.

Jack watched her go, slammed a fist against the steering-wheel, and cursed. He put the vehicle in gear and drove home. Restless despite the late hour and the grueling day they'd had, Jack couldn't sleep. Reaching for the refrigerator door, the kitchen light reflected off his wedding band. He closed the fridge. There was nothing in the damned thing anyway. Instead of trying to seek solace in food, Jack decided a cold shower would be better. It would douse the lust that had seized his body since Maggie Wellington had come to town.

Immersed in the shower, he contemplated the events of the day. The food-poisoning patients would all recover after a few more days of rest. Then Catherine came to mind. He knew she'd suffered through two miscarriages in the past, and this one wasn't going to be any easier for her emotionally, especially with her husband absent. But the spirit healed with time. He knew hers would.

Suddenly Jack frowned, realizing something. Maggie had known Catherine was pregnant. That must have been why they'd traded places at the last minute for the transport. That was Maggie, always putting other people's needs before her own, always there for a friend. Jack closed his eyes and rubbed his hands over his face. His ring scraped his forehead. "Ow," he said. That was the second time he'd noticed the band in just a few minutes. It usually stayed in the background, and he never noticed it.

Without thinking any more about it, he slipped the ring from his finger, reached out of the shower and placed it next to the sink. After he'd finished the shower he rinsed off with cold water. He almost leaped from his skin at the frigid temperature change. He looked down his body. Yep. That ought to work for a while.

Wrapped in a towel, he left the bathroom and entered the bedroom. So many of Arlene's things still lay around. Even the closet held her clothing and shoes he'd never gotten around to packing up.

Jack put on a pair of ratty sweat pants, T-shirt and well-worn trainers. A trip to the garage for a box, and he returned to the bedroom. One by one, he packed away Arlene's belongings. Since they'd had no children, there was no one to save them for. Perhaps Ella would want some of Arlene's collectibles. He'd call her tomorrow to see if she could come over and help.

Lying down on the bed, Jack tried again to sleep, but images of Maggie and their time together at the fish camp swamped his brain, refusing to leave him to the peace he sought.

In a bed across town, Maggie punched her pillow, lay with her head at the foot of the bed and drank hot chocolate, all in the hope of finding a few hours of sleep. Images of Jack kept her from it. Each time she drifted into a light doze she jolted awake, the feel of Jack's body against hers so real she thought he had come back to her.

She rose and took two Benadryl. The clinic prescribed the antihistamine to help people with insomnia without resorting to narcotics. Maggie prayed to the god of sleep to take her under for a few hours—she needed the sleep badly. In the meantime, she dug through her file folder and pulled out the paperwork for CRNA school. In the time it took for Maggie to fill out the first two pages of the application, the Benadryl started to take effect. With a satisfied stretch and a yawn she left the paperwork on the kitchen table and returned to her room. The rest of the references and her résumé could wait until morning.

* * *

Maggie didn't have to be at the hospital, but she wanted to beat Jack over there to check on Catherine. She pulled on a pair of denim shorts, a plain white T-shirt and an Alaska sweatshirt over the top. With her hair pulled into a high swinging ponytail and feet shoved into backless tennis shoes, she was ready. On the way out the door she tucked some money into her pocket and all but skipped to the clinic, refreshed and ready to see Catherine.

The place was quiet for a change. She pushed through the staff doors, looking for Catherine.

"Miss? Can I help you?" Kyle called out to her. "This area is restricted to staff only."

Maggie turned around with a laugh. "Kyle? It's me."

The man staggered and slapped a hand to his chest as he glanced her up and down. "Whoa, Maggie. You look *so-o* different out of uniform. I thought you were a tourist who'd gotten lost." He took her hand and kissed it, and she giggled. "Let me be the first to say thank you."

"For what?" she asked, puzzled.

"For wearing those shorts." He eyed her legs. "Those are a mighty fine set of limbs you got there. Ever use them to hike with?" he asked.

Jack watched the flirtation going on from the doorway. He clenched his jaw and narrowed his eyes. Somehow the pencil in his grip snapped, startling him. He took one step forward, then stopped. He had no claim on Maggie. How many times had he told her so? She could flirt with whomever she wanted. With a laugh she embraced Kyle, and Jack's control broke into pieces like the pencil.

The hell he didn't have any claim on her. Long strides carried him forward.

"Kyle, don't you have patients to check on?"

"I just checked—"

"Yeah. I saw what you were checking." He took Maggie by the arm. "Come with me." He marched her into his office and slammed the door behind them.

"What are you doing?" She jerked her arm from his grip. "You don't have any right to treat me this way."

"You were causing a distraction in the middle of the clinic," he said, and tossed the broken pencil pieces into the trash can.

"I came to check on Catherine."

"She's gone home already."

"Fine. Then I'll just go to her house." She started toward the door.

"Guess you can go back to Kyle now. Sorry I interrupted."

"What the hell are you talking about? Interrupted what?"

Jack crossed the room. "I saw you, Maggie. I saw how he looked at you. He has no right to look at you like that. No right to touch you like that." Jack's hands clenched into fists, and he longed to do something useful with them, like bash them into Kyle's face.

"Did you happen to notice how I looked at him?"

"What?" Jack shook his head, trying to clear the anger from it.

"I looked at him like I look at Jamie. Like a brother. There's nothing sexual between us, but that's none of your business, is it? And as you won't make it your business, leave me alone."

"Before you go, here's your paycheck." He reached into his desk and pulled out an envelope, then opened the door for her to leave.

Maggie took the envelope from him and tore it open. She frowned as she looked at her paycheck. "Jack, this is wrong. It's way too much money."

He took it from her, glanced at it and handed it back to her. "It's correct. Look at the hours worked."

Maggie read it again and frowned. "I still don't understand."

"You got time and a half for the transport and the time at the fish camp."

Maggie stared at him as if he'd lost his mind. "You paid me to have sex with you!"

Jack yanked her back into the office and slammed the door again. "No, I didn't pay you to have sex with me. You get time and a half for the transport until you return home again, however long that takes—that's the policy. We were gone for two days. And keep your voice down. Someone could hear you."

"So what? I'm through doing what people tell me to do because it's uncomfortable not to or because it's proper. I've had enough! I'll tell anyone I want that we had sex. In fact, I think I'll take an ad out in the newspaper. They even have pictures of us together so it should be easy." Maggie reached for the door.

But Jack was faster. He caught her by the arm and spun her around to face him. Without thinking, he smashed through the restraint that he'd kept around himself since he met Miss Maggie Wellington. His arms flashed out and brought her against him, molding her to his body, the fit more perfect than anything else in life.

"You are mine." With a growl, primitive sounding even to him, he captured her mouth with his. The taste of her was pure wild Alaska honey. She met his ferocity with her own, grinding her lips against his. She met the thrust of his tongue with hers. Her hands fisted in his hair, refusing to release her hold on him. Jack backed them against the wall of the office. He held Maggie there, plundering her mouth, memorizing every scent, texture and sound of her as he claimed her for himself.

He broke away from her mouth and seared kisses down her neck, irritated that clothing barred her skin from his. The reaction of his body was swift and fierce, straining against his zipper. If he could rip off Maggie's clothes, he'd take her there against the wall in his office, regardless of anyone who might hear them, and spend himself inside her until they were both drained and satisfied.

As if coming back into his body, his movements slowed, and he noticed Maggie's ragged breathing. He looked at her face, and he pulled back as he noticed tears. In that moment he knew without question that he loved her. How in God's name was he going to live with that? How was he going to live without it? For her sake, he had to let her go. With hands that trembled, he cupped her face.

Maggie hiccuped and tried to control her tears.

"I'm sorry. It won't happen again."

Looking miserable, Maggie pulled away from him and grabbed a tissue from a box on his desk. "God, Jack. Can't you see that I love you? It's written all over me every time we're together." She wiped her face.

"You think you love me," he said, her words twisting in his gut, more painful than any knife wound.

"You idiot. I know I love you. The sad part is that you won't meet me even halfway." She opened the door and looked at him, her eyes filled with sorrow and pain. "Goodbye, Jack. I'll give you my resignation by the end of the day." She turned down a hall away from the main clinic, Kyle and other potential witnesses.

By the time Jack had settled himself enough to go after Maggie, she'd disappeared. Without thought as to the consequences, he raced after her, assuming she'd have gone home. So many times he'd just entered Ella's house without knocking, but he hesitated now at the threshold. Should he just go in and have it out with Maggie or walk away from her for ever?

But as he went to knock on the door it opened, and Maggie stood before him. She reached out and took his hand in hers. "I'm sorry I yelled at you."

"Maggie…" He looked up at her and in that moment he knew he had to tell her he loved her and claim her for himself. How could he? Yet how could he not love the courage and humor and all the things that made her Maggie? He lifted his hand and gently stroked her cheek. "I can't help myself, Maggie, but I love you. God, help me, I do."

"Jack? You're just distraught. This isn't real, it's not true." She began to move away from him but his grip on her hand made her stay.

"No. You've at last managed to open my eyes all the way. I do love you, but—"

"Stop right there," she interrupted, and placed her fingers on his lips. "Say it again."

"I love you," Jack said. Yet inside sadness plagued him. What about Arlene?

"I know you've held yourself back. And I don't want you to give up anything for me."

"What do you mean?" He frowned, but hope flared to life in his heart.

"Your love is big enough for both Arlene and me. If you'll let me, I'd like to know her." She stroked his hair.

Jack clasped her against him as his vision blurred. "I'd like that." He took an unsteady breath and blew out all the doubts, the worries, and the guilt. "I do love you."

"I love you, too."

"I don't know what kind of future we can have, but I'll work on it with you." He stood and looked down at the table beside her. With a frown, he noticed the paperwork she had been working on. "What's this?"

"An application for school." She took the papers from his hands and stacked them to one side.

"School? You were going to leave without telling me?" He could hardly believe this was happening.

"Jack, sit down." Maggie frowned and tried to urge him into a chair.

"I don't need to sit down. I need some answers." His heart raced in his chest. Had he just been delusional a moment ago? "You can't leave."

"As usual, you're jumping to conclusions. A huge one this time. I'm *not leaving*," she said, and groaned through gritted teeth. "Now, sit down and listen to me for just a minute," she said, and shoved him into a chair.

"I *do* want to go to school. CRNA school. But it's going to take me a year to go through the process and get accepted. So I won't be going anywhere for a while."

Jack raked his fingers through his hair. "But you'll still leave, won't you?"

The sorrow in his eyes almost brought Maggie to her knees. "Yes."

"Well, I guess that's the end of it, isn't it?" he said, and stood. "I knew—"

"I'd hoped that you'd come with me." Maggie chewed on her lower lip, hesitation and vulnerability on her face.

Jack stopped at the door and turned. "Come with you?"

"Yes. To Seattle. That's where I'm going to school. Your family's there, and I had hoped that you would want to see them again, maybe make a home with me."

"Make a home with you?" Jack blinked as the blinders fell away from his eyes. For good.

"Yes. Then we could come back. You've talked endlessly about not having anyone to run anesthesia. After I graduate, I could do it. We could run the clinic together, Jack." She moved toward him, her steps slow, hesitant. "That is, if you want me. If you love me and want to make a life with me."

Before Maggie realized he had moved, Jack was holding her against him. "Of course I want you. I've spent the last few weeks trying not to, but I just can't be with you and not want you any longer. I don't care who knows any more. I love you, Maggie. I love you."

Her hands clutched his, and her eyes went wide. "You took off your ring," she whispered.

"I did. It was the right time." He kissed her hard, then drew back. "I want to make a place in my life for you if you'll have me. In my heart. All of it."

Tears flooded Maggie's eyes. "Jack." She breathed

his name. "I don't know what the future holds, but I want one with you in it. I love you. I've loved you since the trip to the fish camp. I know you had to leave me behind, and I loved you for coming back for me."

"I was so scared for you, but I didn't know why until now. You've made my life worth living again, Maggie. I'll be forever grateful to you for that." He smiled and his time it reached all the way to his eyes.

"Grateful?" Maggie stepped back as the smile dropped from her face and apprehension curled in her stomach.

"Yes. I believe it's important to thank people when they do good deeds."

"I've just bared my soul to you, and you're *grateful* to me? Oh, God. This is so humiliating." Maggie hung her head.

Jack placed his hands on her shoulders. "I am grateful, Maggie. Because it made me realize how much I love you and what an idiot I've been in not seeing how much you love me, too."

She looked up at him and met his gaze, seeing the truth in his words. "Would you put another ring on your hand?"

"Only if it's yours," he said, and kissed her.

EPILOGUE

MAGGIE shivered, but whether it was from nerves or the cold she couldn't tell. A wintry wind ruffled her full-length white coat. Matching boots warmed her feet beneath the ivory lace gown. Flowers didn't last long in the cold air, so Maggie carried a bundle of silk calla lilies.

Catherine fussed at her one more time, adjusting the wreath of flowers and cascade of ringlets dripping from Maggie's crown.

"It's been quite a year, hasn't it?" Catherine smiled. She was so pleased that Maggie had found the happiness she deserved.

"Yes, for us both." Maggie reached out to hug her friend and had to accommodate the woman's enlarged belly. Catherine's dreams were also coming true with a viable pregnancy.

"You are the most beautiful bride I've ever seen," Catherine whispered, and wiped tears from her eyes. "I cry at everything these days, but they are happy tears for you."

"Thank you," Maggie said, and looked away from her friend up at the bright blue sky. Winter was arrived, crisp and clear, providing six hours of brilliant sunshine. Today Maggie's special day seemed blessed with even more. It was welcome in the midst of a winter carnival.

"Are you ready?" Jamie asked as he fluffed his coat and stamped his feet, trying to stay warm.

"Yes."

"No doubts?"

"None whatsoever," Maggie said, and gave a smile to Jamie.

"Then, little sister, I think there's someone waiting for you."

"Take me to him," she said, and tucked her arm into the crook of his.

Jamie helped Maggie into the waiting dog sled and climbed in behind her. "Let's go, Ella," he said.

"You got it. Hike!" she called to the team of eight Alaskan sled dogs. They pulled together and the sled shot forward through the snow.

Ella mushed them through the village and past the church, too small to accommodate all the guests. Everyone who knew the couple wanted to offer good wishes for their future together.

The winter carnival had begun. Ice sculptures of mermaids, whales, fishermen and wolves were scattered around the area, giving an otherworldly ambiance to the day.

The small group arrived at a castle of ice that took center stage. Guests milled around, admiring the sculptures and drinking hot coffee, but everyone turned as the sled came to a stop.

Jamie jumped out and then offered Maggie his hand as she stepped out of the sled. "Ready?"

"Definitely." She nodded, smiling. From the entrance of the castle Jack stood only twenty feet away, the light in his eyes only for her.

The music began, and Maggie clutched Jamie's arm as they walked down the aisle of ice to her man. Jamie gave her over to Jack, who leaned down and whispered into her ear, "I love you, Maggie."

"No kissing before the pronouncement," the minister said with a grin.

"Then hurry, because I want to kiss her. A lot," Jack replied, and those close enough to hear chuckled.

Maggie and Jack recited their vows, binding their lives together.

After the ceremony the festivities moved indoors, and Jamie took Maggie aside. "Father sent a present," he said, and drew a long envelope from beneath his coat.

Maggie shook her head, trying not to let old emotions take hold. "I don't want his money," she said.

"Good, because you aren't getting it." He put the envelope into her hands. "This is the first installment for the free clinic you want to build."

Maggie clutched Jamie to her. "Oh! You did it. Thank you," she cried.

"This was all you, little sister. If you hadn't asked, it wouldn't have happened."

As Maggie wiped away a tear, Jack approached. "Jamie, why are you making my bride cry on our wedding day?"

She turned and smiled up at her new husband, handing him the envelope.

Jack quickly scanned the document and pulled Maggie into his arms. "You are an angel, my angel," he said.

"Yours and only yours," Maggie said, and kissed him.